DEBRA OSWALD is a writer for stage, film, television and children's fiction.

Debra's stageplays have been produced around Australia. *Gary's House*, *Sweet Road* and *The Peach Season* were all shortlisted for the NSW Premier's Award. Her play *Dags* has had many Australian productions and has been published and performed in Britain and the United States. *Gary's House* has been on the senior high school syllabus and has been performed in Denmark in translation. *The Peach Season* won the 2005 Seaborn Playwright's Prize. *Mr Bailey's Minder* broke the Griffin Theatre's box office record in 2004, toured nationally in 2006 and will be produced in Philadelphia in 2008.

Debra has written two plays for the Australian Theatre for Young People: *Skate*, performed in Sydney, on a NSW country tour and at the Belfast Theatre Festival. *Stories in the Dark* will premiere at Riverside Theatre Parramatta in 2007.

She is the author of three 'Aussie Bite' books for kids, including *Nathan and the Ice Rockets*, and five novels for teenage readers: *Me and Barry Terrific*, *The Return of the Baked Bean*, *The Fifth Quest*, *The Redback Leftovers* and *Getting Air*.

Among Debra's television credits are *Bananas in Pyjamas*, *Sweet and Sour*, *Palace of Dreams*, *The Secret Life of Us* and award-winning episodes of *Police Rescue*.

Anne Looby (seated) as Celia and Maeve Dermody as Zoe in the 2006 Griffin Theatre Company production in Sydney. (Photo: Robert McFarlane)

The Peach Season

DEBRA OSWALD

Currency Press, Sydney

CURRENCY PLAYS

First published in 2007
by Currency Press Pty Ltd,
PO Box 2287, Strawberry Hills, NSW, 2012, Australia
enquiries@currency.com.au
www.currency.com.au

NATIONAL LIBRARY OF AUSTRALIA CIP DATA

    Oswald, Debra.
        The peach season.
        For secondary school students.
        ISBN 9780868198057.
        I. Title.
    A822.3

Publication of this title was assisted by the Commonwealth Government through the Australia Council, its arts funding and advisory body.

Printed by Ligare Pty Ltd, Riverwood, NSW.
Cover design by Kate Florance, Currency Press.

Front cover shows Maeve Dermody as Zoe and Scott Timmins as Keiran. Back cover shows Maeve Dermody as Zoe and Anne Looby as Celia. Both from the 2006 Griffin Theatre Company premiere production. (Photos: Robert McFarlane)

Contents

For Annabelle Sheehan

Introduction

Maeve Dermody

*The instant a person loves a person or a thing, they face the risk
of losing that person or thing.*

Dorothy; Act One, Scene One.

The risk of actual and potential loss in the face of loving another human
being, with all its weight of anxiety and fear, is the force that drives
the adult characters of *The Peach Season*. The young can't yet dream
of it, and the old have learned to manage it, but those in the middle
are still struggling to carry its burden without distorting their love. In
deeply human fashion the characters trip over and make mistakes as
they struggle with the painfulness of loving and being loved. And yet,
Debra Oswald's gift is utter intimacy and honesty in the sharing of
these relationships with the audience, which are so familiar that we
cannot judge or condemn them.

Explored through a set of several of the most momentous or
archetypal relationships we humans experience—mother/daughter,
mother/son, brother/sister—loss and the fear of loss are seen in the
play as damaging, and all but unavoidable, but something that we have
no choice but to endure and survive. Finally, we must learn to hold
these two opposing pulls inside the power of love together.

This big and universally understandable emotional canvas, set in a
peach orchard at picking time, was brought to life for the first time by
Griffin Theatre Company at The Stables Theatre in 2006—one of the
smallest stages in Sydney. I was fortunate to work closely with Debra
Oswald in the premiere production when I played Zoe, Celia's sixteen-
year-old daughter, whose powerful but barely conscious need to tear
herself away from her mother, drives much of the dramatic action of
the play.

Zoe is driven to take big risks, and rip herself away from Celia because
her margin of permissible risk has always been too tightly monitored,

however lovingly, by the concern of her mother. In the swift, lustful, exquisite excitement of falling for Kieran, the lovable no-hoper, she is freed her from her burden of responsibly living her life so entirely inside the boundaries of Celia's intense anxiety for her.

Kieran is an endearing loose cannon, damaged by former drug use, but genuinely sweet in his unhindered enthusiasm and frankness, unaware of boundaries, free of censorship, irresistible to Zoe. Forbidden fruit she must taste. His unrestricted openness to life, which makes him dangerous to himself, lets her find and let that loose in herself. It makes him 'the most alive person' she has ever met, and enables her to feel 'whole' for the first time in her life.

This provides the incision point to cut herself free from Celia's smothering concern for her, which overruns Zoe's boundaries in a way she increasingly senses as unlivable, unacceptable. She comes to resent the way she has always had to behave in a way to preserve the careful world Celia has set up to shelter herself and her child from the devastating grief of unexpectedly losing her husband when Zoe was a baby. This quiet compensation made for another's pain is mirrored in the character of Joe, Dorothy's son, who has had to navigate around his own mother's unspoken trauma of war and loss. While it may have been acceptable to a child willing to please, Zoe is herself at that point of blooming into ripeness, right when the peaches are ready for picking—and short of pickers.

One critic commented that Anne Looby's Celia was 'tightly coiled', and indeed it is only when the unravelling begins that the full weight of the unspoken load of Celia's loss and fear of more loss, that Zoe has been lugging all her life, becomes wholly evident. But the complexity of this emotion made it very hard for me, as Zoe, to find a way to completely validate the hate that flies from her towards her mum. Celia is motivated purely by maternal love, and by what she feels sure is best and safest for Zoe. Such richly conflicted feelings as this play presents again and again are a wonderful, difficult gift to an actor, and I'm sure for an audience also.

Like the bruising of fruit handled roughly in its bloom, loosening this stranglehold of mother love is painful for both of them, but is of course inevitable: Zoe must lose her innocence and come into her own in order to gain her life—her own set of experiences through a first wild assertion of independence. Celia must learn that the final act or lesson of love is letting go, granting freedom to the one who is so loved, and trusting that they will be safe. The poignancy of the situation is heralded from the beginning of the play in the Eden-like setting of the peach orchard, with its rapidly ripening fruit and thick summer heat. Celia's careful Eden proves hugely vulnerable to the arrival of Kieran and Sheena, with their edgy, urban, damaged energy. As these forces build, so does the heat, which with the rain threatens to 'cook' the perfect peaches on the trees.

This is just a small part of Debra's skill as playwright: she fosters a delicately charged symbolic tonality inside a completely realistic realm. She also uses archetypal themes to frame the lives of complex, faulty, fundamentally ordinary people—hugely resonant material to work with. I found it interesting in rehearsal to lightly draw on the hint in the play of the Demeter and Persephone myth. However, in Debra's work such mythic undertone never breaks the surface nor steals the humanity of her characters, not even for a moment. The myth begins with the ultimate image in Greek myth of a deeply-bonded mother-daughter pair. In the more familiar version, this myth tells of Persephone's violent abduction by Hades, Lord of the Underworld, but in the earliest, pre-Hellenic telling of the myth, the daughter, Persephone, is drawn consciously and even willingly into the darkness of the Underworld. She senses that the Shades of the Underworld need a breath of life-awareness, just as the upper world needs intimate knowledge of death. Darkness is sought in a way that is similar to Zoe when she disappears with Kieran at the end of the first Act. Indeed, most glimpses of Zoe in the second half of the play are in partial darkness, and shadows; she is inside the alluring darkness which she has always had restricted access to, concealed as much as possible by Celia.

This culminates in her description to Sheena, towards the end of the play, of the primal scene of utter violence that she has witnessed and only barely survived—a crossfire scene similar to that which snatched her father's life when she was an infant. Zoe, whose name, of course, means 'life', has all but deliberately visited and taken into herself the dark scene of death and violence she could never glimpse for herself, but which has been powerfully and tightly organising her life up to that point.

At this point Sheena is the only person who can really hear what Zoe has witnessed because she has lived a life as regular spectator to a similar form of uninhibited darkness in people. She is a juxtaposing character to Zoe: bought up without a real mother figure, and forced to develop sharp, strong edges to protect herself. And yet, her exposure to harshness means she remains deeply loyal to the true decency she can see so clearly in Kieran. This is why she offers tough, big-sisterly concern for him, and an alternative mother figure.

In the myth, Demeter, goddess of harvest and fertility, goes crazy with grief and fear, not knowing where her daughter has gone. Her season of despair infects the entire world in the death of crops and an endlessly prolonged winter. In Act Two, the bright summer light of the first Act is replaced with dim winter light, and the stage was scattered with a huge pile of dead leaves. The orchard is dull and untended in an endless winter that can be broken, finally, only with reassurance of Zoe's existence once again.

With this shift of season, the rhythm and tone of the play also slows, and fragments, holding stylistically the weight of everything falling apart thematically in the lives of the characters. This shift, which shows Debra is not being dictated to by a uniform use of coherent dramatic conventions, is very exciting to work inside. We were particularly privileged in the rehearsal process, where she consistently adapted the rhythm and movement of parts of the dialogue in this section, to what was developing emotionally for the actors, and to David Berthold's perceptive stage direction.

One particular area that was constantly reworked was the degree of direct address utilised. In Act One, only Dorothy connects explicitly with the audience. She is threaded in and out of the main action, chorus-like, and provides much of the comic relief. She is in a way similar to the figure of Hecate, the wise crone of the Demeter and Persephone myth. She has accumulated wisdom and a measure of human acceptance which allows her to be more prescient. In the myth, Hecate knows where Persephone has been snatched to, but calmly lets it continue, at least long enough for both mother and daughter to get some painful wisdom born of holding the opposites, rather than holding them at bay.

But from the beginning in the second Act both Celia and Sheena also communicate face-to-face with the audience. All three women intersect with and spur on the thoughts and words of each other. They remain the solid weave of concern and information about the dramatic action. Quite often they remain onstage in the relatively brief glimpses of Zoe and Kieran, who stay more separate and unreachable. Scott Timmins (who played Kieran) and I deliberately kept detached, both on and off stage, from the others throughout our first scenes of Act Two. Most nights we ran pell-mell through the back streets of Kings Cross, which surround the theatre. We kept pushing the limit of how much time we left before we got to the bottom of the stage, ready for our first cue to enter. When we did enter we were willed back into being and up onto the stage by the forceful exchange of dialogue between Celia and Dorothy that cues our entrance, and carried real adrenaline into our dark city scenes. Running fast up and down the precipitous stairwell of the Stables Theatre that forms one of the two possible stage exits was also enough to keep our edginess and energy very high.

Darkness comes to be held inside light by the end of the play. While it might seem somewhat tidy in its resolution, what is important is that Zoe is now allowed to make her own mistakes, and Celia can see how beautiful this makes her. Kieran, as her dear companion, has led her to places which were crucial for her to discover, and which she will have no choice but to continue to explore for the rest of her life. Zoe holds this experience of the underworld in her private mental and emotional life, evident to others only occasionally when it shows through as 'a darkness in her voice'.

This is not unlike Persephone who, in the myth, forms an agreement with Hades to live three months of the year in the Underworld and the other nine months on earth with her mother. Because of her experiences she is able to see with the eyes of death.

Zoe and Celia are bound together by their shared but unspoken knowledge of death and loss. It brings them into a more adult closeness. This is so poignant in the final image of the play. As Zoe stretches and opens, Celia speaks of her resoluteness to transform what was once deep panic, into an energy which protects. It is an energy forged through a trust of the stunning strength in Zoe, which took her so long to truly see.

The Peach Season is a generous and intimate experience by a playwright who holds nothing back. Debra is deeply attuned to what we love in each other as human beings: the passion, the contradictions, the unceasing dedication to one and other. In knowing people, she knows actors and knows an audience. Her work encompasses both great humour and real anguish. David Berthold, our director in the first production, shares Debra's innate understanding of humanness, and effortlessly translated it from the written material to the stage. The audience is so close on The Stables stage that you cannot get away with anything but pure emotional honesty and all the performances were sincere and sensitive to this.

I was deeply proud to be part of a play where, by the end, all the actors and audience members had truly navigated the same terrain together, and all carried the world of the play inside them. By the end of the play it often seemed that everyone was red-eyed and exhausted, and yet truly exhilarated. Surely this is what theatre at its very best is all about.

Maeve Dermody is an actor who appeared as Zoe in the Griffin Theatre Company premiere of The Peach Season *in 2006.*

Demeter and Persephone

Debra Oswald

The myth of Demeter and Persephone exists in many forms and with many variations, from pagan legend, Greek myth, Homer, Ovid, Tennyson, through to very recent reinterpretations of the story.

Demeter was the goddess of the crops and the harvest, keeping the earth abundant with growing things and plenty to eat. She had one daughter, Persephone, known as the Maiden of Spring. Lovely Persephone made Demeter's heart sing and the goddess liked to keep her daughter close. But as Persephone grew older, she grew curious about the world and eager to explore beyond her mother's watchful gaze.

One morning Persephone was collecting flowers in a meadow. The beautiful narcissus flower caught her eye and to get a closer look she wandered deeper into the forest. Suddenly the ground under her feet began to tremble and a huge chasm opened up. Out from the gaping hole in the ground came a chariot drawn by mighty black horses. Hades, the god of the Underworld, ruler of the Kingdom of the Dead, had been watching Persephone. He had fallen desperately in love with her. Hades pulled Persephone into his chariot and sped away into the shadows. Persephone cried out but quickly the earth closed over her, leaving no trace.

When Demeter discovered her daughter was missing, she was overcome with grief, refusing to eat or bathe. She wandered the earth, searching for her daughter, but could find no sign of her. Finally, she was met by Hecate, the old woman goddess of the crossroads, known as the Queen of the Night, mysterious and wise. The crone Hecate told Demeter that she had heard Persephone's cries as she disappeared into the Underworld. It broke Demeter's heart to think of her precious daughter trapped in the shadowy Kingdom of the Dead.

And so for many months, the angry goddess neglected the crops and refused to allow the earth to bloom. Every growing thing withered and died, the once green fields became barren and people were dying of starvation across the lands.

The danger was that all humankind would be destroyed, so Zeus stepped in to solve the problem. Zeus tried to negotiate between his brother Hades and Demeter. Finally Hades agreed to allow Persephone to leave the Underworld. However Hades knew she would have to return to him because Persephone had eaten seven seeds from a pomegranate. Anyone who has eaten food while in the Underworld is doomed to return there.

Eventually a compromise was reached: it was decided that Persephone would spend three months of the year in the Underworld, ruling alongside Hades, and then spend the other nine months living on the earth with her mother.

When Persephone and Demeter were reunited, there were tears of joy. During her time in the Underworld, Persephone had learned the mysteries of death and darkness, emerging stronger and forever changed. She could no longer look at a beautiful flower in bloom without also imagining its withered decaying fate. There were no more carefree summer days full of laughter and innocence.

Every year, during the months Persephone stays in the Underworld, the goddess Demeter mourns and makes the earth barren and cold, allowing little to grow. Then when Persephone returns to her mother each spring, the earth blooms again with fertility, warmth and abundance.

Sydney
April 2007

ACKNOWLEDGEMENTS

Debra Oswald would like to thank Christopher Hurrell, Michael Wynne, Richard Glover, Campion Decent, Kerry Laurence, Les Langlands, Dr Rodney Seaborn and the Seaborn Broughton Walford Foundation, Stephen Collins, Sydney Theatre Company, Griffin Theatre, David Berthold, the cast and creative team of the Griffin production.

The Peach Season was first produced by Griffin Theatre Company at the SBW Stables, Sydney, on 15 March 2006, with the following cast:

CELIA	Anne Looby
DOROTHY	Maggie Blinco
ZOE	Maeve Dermody
JOE	John Adam
SHEENA	Alice Parkinson
KIERAN	Scott Timmins

Director, David Berthold
Designer, Alice Babidge
Lighting Designer, Stephen Hawker
Sound Design, Jeremy Silver

CHARACTERS

CELIA
DOROTHY
ZOE
JOE
SHEENA
KIERAN

ACT ONE

SCENE ONE

A stone-fruit farm. Summer.

Trees heavy with fruit. Palettes of packing boxes in a yard which is flanked by a house and sheds.

CELIA *enters with her arms full of peaches. She is in her early forties, energetic, warm.*

CELIA: Have you seen these Red Havens?! Luscious. Dead-on ready to pick. A day over, if anything.

> *She gently releases the armload of fruit into a box. We realise she is speaking to* DOROTHY.

> DOROTHY *is in her seventies, with a Hungarian accent. She wears an assortment of vibrantly patterned clothes and a mass of long grey hair. She can wander between scenes—sometimes in the scene herself, sometimes addressing the audience.*

DOROTHY: [*to the audience*] Before we begin this story, let me say: you can't put the blame to anyone for what happened. Good people. Trying to avoid the necessary losses.

CELIA: Zoe fell asleep after lunch.

DOROTHY: Ah.

CELIA: I won't wake her up now. She might as well sleep while I work out what to do. [*She grabs a peach from the box and inhales its scent. She laughs.*] Can you believe this? Best season for five years and the bloody fruit's going to rot on the trees.

> CELIA *throws herself into work, hauling stuff around.*

> *Sixteen-year-old* ZOE *appears, unseen by* CELIA, *and watches from a hiding spot.*

DOROTHY: [*to the audience*] Sometimes all you can do is sit back and watch people make mistakes. The instant a person loves a person or a thing, they face the risk of losing that person or thing.

JOE *enters, taking off his suit coat and rolling up his shirt sleeves. He's about forty.*

CELIA: Joe! Hi. Want a cold drink on this stinking day?

JOE: Nah, I'm fine, thanks.

DOROTHY: He's driven in his airconditioned car from his airconditioned office.

JOE: How are you, Mum?

JOE *gives* DOROTHY *a kiss on both cheeks.*

DOROTHY: Why do you come out here to check on me? I'm okay.

JOE: I'm here to maybe do Celia a favour. Are you still needing pickers?

CELIA: Desperately. Roy's whole mob of pickers have buggered off nobody knows where.

JOE *signals to someone offstage.* KIERAN *and* SHEENA *enter.*

JOE: I might've found you a couple of people.

CELIA *watches them approach.* KIERAN *is eighteen, ebullient, hyper, gauche, but winning.* SHEENA, *in her mid-twenties, has a tough, sharp-tongued manner, awkward and wary.*

CELIA: You know them?

JOE: No. They were at the garage in town. Car broken down.

CELIA: [*smiling heartily*] G'day. I'm Celia.

SHEENA: Oh, uh, Sheena and this is—

KIERAN: Kieran. Celia? Celia? Hi. This place is so mad. The trees right down to the road— You grew all those?

CELIA: Yeah.

KIERAN: Mad. All this excellent fruit.

KIERAN *grins at* CELIA *who can't help smiling back.*

CELIA: Oh, this is Joe's mum, Dorothy.

SHEENA *nods hello.*

Dorothy handles the fruit grading and packing for us at this time of year.

DOROTHY: [*dancing her hands in the air*] The sharpest eyes and softest hands available in the fruit bowl of south-western New South Wales.

KIERAN *laughs, appreciating* DOROTHY. *While* SHEENA *and* CELIA *talk,* KIERAN *bounces around looking at the peaches with delighted curiosity.*

SHEENA: Heard you might have some work going.

CELIA: Yeah.

SHEENA: Well, we need to earn some money as quickly as we can so—umm—

CELIA: Any experience picking stone fruit?

> SHEENA *shakes her head.*

Any kind of fruit?

SHEENA: None.

CELIA: Okay. That's teachable. That's doable. When your car's fixed, you'll have transport out here from town every day?

SHEENA: Uh, no, we don't get the car back 'til we earn the money to pay for the parts.

CELIA: Right… It's just we're not set up to have pickers stay on the place.

> JOE *draws* CELIA *aside for a whispered conference.*

JOE: They're pretty desperate, I reckon. Any chance they could camp on the property?

CELIA: I don't like the idea of people—strangers—staying out here. I decided years ago not to go that way.

JOE: Yep, fair enough. If you don't feel comfortable about it, I'll find them somewhere else to—

SHEENA: Look, um, if it's all a big hassle, y'know, don't worry. We'll piss off and—

CELIA: No. Don't piss off. I've got twenty thousand peaches that have to be picked before they rot. I need hard workers in a hurry.

SHEENA: I need two thousand bucks in a hurry.

> CELIA *looks at* SHEENA, *sizing her up.*

CELIA: See that shack? It's primitive. And filthy. Hasn't been used for fifteen years.

SHEENA: Primitive is okay.

CELIA: We can clean it out, I'm sure.

JOE: Anything I can do to help?

CELIA: We just need to scrounge up some stuff to make the place decent. [*To* DOROTHY] Can you start explaining to Kieran how we pick?

SHEENA: Kieran. Remember. Don't be a dickhead.

KIERAN *nods resolutely.* CELIA, SHEENA *and* JOE *exit together.*

KIERAN: Is it hard? Picking peaches?

DOROTHY: Hard work. If you want to earn decent money. Oh, yes.

KIERAN: I mean, hard like difficult.

DOROTHY *grabs* KIERAN's *hands and inspects them.*

DOROTHY: You'll be okay.

KIERAN: You can tell from my hands?

DOROTHY: This contraption is a picking bag.

KIERAN: Cool.

DOROTHY: How tall are you?

She measures his upper body with her hands.

I must adjust the strap before we start.

She fiddles with the strap.

KIERAN: So do you live here, Dorothy?

DOROTHY: No. I live in the yellow house down there at the crossroad. On my own since Sandor died.

KIERAN: Your husband?

DOROTHY: He died since eight years.

KIERAN: Oh, I'm sorry. Hey—what country are you from originally?

DOROTHY: Hungary.

KIERAN: Yeah? Far out. Did you come out here—?

DOROTHY: Many years ago.

DOROTHY *makes a dismissive gesture—she doesn't want to talk about it.*

KIERAN: This is an awesome place. So beautiful. And bulk peaches on tap! Oh—guess you get sick of eating peaches.

DOROTHY: Not so much. Because the season ends and then by the time it comes around again you think—oh, peaches would be nice.

KIERAN: Right. I get you.

DOROTHY: Try one of the Red Havens.

KIERAN: Oh—we allowed to eat them?

DOROTHY: This one's got a split. So you might as well.

KIERAN *bites into the peach and gasps, getting a rush.*

KIERAN: Oh, this is—far out, this is— How come I never tasted anything like this in my life before?

DOROTHY: Because you only ever ate those green bullety excuses for peaches they sell in supermarkets in the city. You never had a Red Haven fresh from the tree.

KIERAN *eats the peach with noisy, messy gusto, juice all over his face and hands. Without taking her eyes off the picking bag she's adjusting,* DOROTHY *calls out.*

[*Calling*] Are you going to hide over there and spy on us all afternoon?

KIERAN: Sorry?

KIERAN *spins around with mock paranoia.*

Are you, like, a mental old lady? Or is there really someone spying on us?

DOROTHY: Zoe.

ZOE *comes out from her hiding place.*

ZOE: How come you always know where I am?

DOROTHY: From the corner in my eye, I see you moving a little. Restless, ants on your pants, watching everything that goes on.

ZOE: [*affectionately*] The same as you, Mrs Stickybeak.

DOROTHY *laughs and grabs* ZOE's *face, proprietorial.*

DOROTHY: This is Zoe.

KIERAN: Oh. Right. Hi. Hi. Kieran. I'm Kieran.

KIERAN *leaps forward and offers his hand to shake.* ZOE, *startled, shakes his hand and discovers it's sticky.*

ZOE: Oh.

KIERAN: Ah! Sorry. Peach juice.

KIERAN *laughs and licks the peach juice off his hand.*

SHEENA, *carrying cleaning gear, emerges from the house to find* KIERAN *licking his hand like a hyperactive dog.*

SHEENA: Kieran. Are you acting like a head case and driving this lady crazy?

KIERAN: No. Oh well, maybe— Am I?

DOROTHY: He's okay.

KIERAN: Oh. Oh. Sheena, this is Zoe.

SHEENA: Hello.

KIERAN: Zoe might think I'm a head case. Do you, Zoe?

> SHEENA *drags* KIERAN *away, whispering to him sternly.* KIERAN *keeps smiling, eyes fixed on* ZOE.

> CELIA *enters with an armload of bedding.*

CELIA: [*to* ZOE] Ah, you're awake, Sleeping Beauty. You still look a bit sleepy.

ZOE: I thought, 'I'll close my eyes for one second', then I flaked.

CELIA: You worked hard this morning.

ZOE: I jerked awake. Realised I'd dribbled a bit on the couch... errgh.

CELIA: Errgh, yeah. I hate that feeling. [*To* KIERAN] How are you getting on?

KIERAN: Heaps good. Tasted a sample of your peaches. Awesome.

CELIA: Thanks. Kieran, this is my daughter—

KIERAN: Zoe.

> *The way* KIERAN *says her name makes* ZOE *start.*

ZOE: We—uh—met a second ago.

CELIA: Oh. Right. Great.

DOROTHY: [*handing* CELIA *the picking bag*] I can't move the bloody bastard strap.

CELIA: It's tricky, this one. [*To* KIERAN *and* SHEENA] Can I show you how we use these?

> *While* DOROTHY *addresses the audience,* CELIA *demonstrates to* KIERAN *and* SHEENA *how to fill a picking bag with peaches, then release the bottom of the cloth bag so the peaches roll gently into a bin.* ZOE *makes a show of being busy with something but she sneaks looks at* KIERAN.

DOROTHY: [*to the audience*] When Celia came to this farm with baby Zoe, the story went whoosh around the district about Celia's husband. He was buying milk at a service station—this is in the city, before Celia came here, when Celia was pregnant with Zoe. There was a robbery at the service station. With a gun. Celia's husband, standing by the fridges, was killed. So. Celia bought this farm. People around here thought she was crazy. 'She can't run the place on her own.' But I saw Celia was a strong woman. Robust.

> JOE *enters.*

JOE: Zoe. G'day. Didn't see you there. All done with school for the year?

ZOE: Yep. Eight weeks off. They design the school terms around the picking season, so I'm here and Mum can work me like a slave.

CELIA *pretends to lash* ZOE *who cowers like a beaten slave.* ZOE *loses her balance, laughs.* CELIA *catches her fall.*

JOE: [*to* DOROTHY] I'll drop by again this week. So if there's anything you want from town—

DOROTHY: I say again—you don't have to come out here and check on me.

JOE *exchanges a look with* CELIA—*both of them are used to* DOROTHY. DOROTHY *sidles across to* KIERAN *and* SHEENA *and in a whisper designed to be audible:*

He would do better to be checking on his marriage.

CELIA: How's Fiona?

JOE: Good, thanks. Yeah, she's powering along.

DOROTHY: [*to* KIERAN *and* SHEENA] Fiona is the mean-spirited harpy who trapped my son in a marriage with no joy. And who has turned his two children into nasty little snobs who don't respect their own father.

JOE: [*to* CELIA] I got those photos printed up for you.

JOE *and* CELIA *move away from the others to get the photos out of* JOE*'s suit coat.*

Snaps from Zoe's sixteenth.

CELIA *flips through the photos.*

CELIA: Thanks for these. Oh—Zoe looks beautiful in this one.

JOE: You both do.

CELIA: Oh, no.

JOE: Yes.

CELIA *laughs, embarrassed.*

CELIA: You know, I've got photos your dad took of us years ago—me with Zoe in the baby backpack.

She watches JOE *looking at the photos.*

How are you, Joe?

JOE: Fine.

CELIA: I hope you'd tell me if you weren't fine.

JOE: Oh… you know, it's difficult… it's never a simple thing.

CELIA: I understand.

JOE: I'm just trying to do the right thing by everyone. But sometimes I wonder if—

> JOE's *mobile phone rings. He apologises to* CELIA, *then walks away to have a conversation.* CELIA *rejoins the others.*

DOROTHY: [*to* KIERAN *and* SHEENA] That will be her. Fiona. She rings him constantly on the infernal machine. It's her surveillance system. To make sure he's not having any fun.

> CELIA *suppresses a smile and gives* DOROTHY *a stern look.*

CELIA: Dorothy.

KIERAN: Joe's, like, a lawyer or something?

DOROTHY: Solicitor. Very boring, if you ask me. But safe, I suppose. Josef and Fiona—they don't have sex. You can tell when a couple is not having enough sex. The way their bodies are with each other in a room. To live alone and have no sex, that's bad enough. But to be married and have no sex—that corrodes a person's insides eventually and then—

> DOROTHY *shuts up when* JOE *finishes his call.*

JOE: Was my mother saying appalling things?

CELIA: Appalling beyond description. I'll see what we've got that's cold to drink—

JOE: Uh, no, can't stay. Better head straight back into town.

DOROTHY: Ah. Fiona's radar is warning her that Josef might be having a pleasant time.

JOE: Mum. At least do it so I can't hear.

> DOROTHY *presses her lips together and puts her hands up—an innocent party.*

See you Wednesday. [*To* SHEENA *and* KIERAN] Good luck with the picking work.

KIERAN: Thanks, Joe mate.

SHEENA: Uh—yeah—y'know, thanks and everything.

> CELIA *walks a little way with* JOE.

JOE: Give me a yell if you're worried at all or if—

CELIA: Ah, we'll be sweet. Look after yourself, Joe.

> *As* DOROTHY *watches* JOE *go, she addresses the audience.*

DOROTHY: [*to the audience*] Who your child marries—there's nothing you can do about that. Hope for the best. And if the best doesn't happen—if, for example, your son marries Fiona—you can only sigh and keep your mouth shut.

CELIA: [*to* KIERAN *and* SHEENA] Getting the hang of the bags?

KIERAN: Reckon we are. I'm totally amped about this picking thing. Do we start right now?

CELIA: We'll lose the light soon. Best if we start picking first thing tomorrow.

DOROTHY: [*to* CELIA] And best if you ring the markets quick smart.

CELIA: Yeah. Let them know they'll be getting some peaches from me.

> CELIA *goes inside.*

SHEENA: Kieran. Let's get scrubbing.

> SHEENA *indicates the cleaning gear, bedding, etc.*

KIERAN: Oh. Right. Yeah.

> KIERAN *picks up an armload of stuff and follows* SHEENA. *But he walks backwards so he can keep looking at* ZOE. *He stumbles and falls, whooping with laughter.* ZOE *laughs.* SHEENA *gathers up the gear* KIERAN *has sent flying everywhere.*

SHEENA: Sorry about this. Kieran's a bit of a—

KIERAN: A bit of a clueless fuckwit.

> ZOE *hands* KIERAN *some of the stuff he dropped.*

Ta.

> SHEENA *stalks off.* KIERAN *hurries after her, smiling at* ZOE.

CELIA: [*offstage*] Zoe!

ZOE: Coming!

> ZOE *runs inside.* DOROTHY *exits as the daylight fades.*

SCENE TWO

Evening.

CELIA *is still working around the packing shed.* SHEENA *walks up from the shack with cleaning gear.*

CELIA: How you going? Is it fit to live in?
SHEENA: It'll do us. So guess I'll see you, um—
CELIA: Have you and Kieran been on the road a fair while?

> SHEENA *immediately becomes defensive.*

SHEENA: Couple of months.
CELIA: You headed somewhere in particular?
SHEENA: What?
CELIA: Just wondering what you're—
SHEENA: Why? I mean, does it matter?
CELIA: No, I'm sorry. Didn't mean to be nosey. It's none of my—
SHEENA: We're not gonna rob you or anything.
CELIA: Christ, I wasn't meaning—
SHEENA: Kieran and me want to earn some money and then move on.
CELIA: Of course. I was only—
SHEENA: I know my brother comes across a bit weird.
CELIA: Brother?
SHEENA: Well, half-brother.
CELIA: Oh.
SHEENA: I mean, if you got a problem with us being here—
CELIA: Sorry… I thought you and Kieran were together.
SHEENA: Together together? A couple? Kieran's eighteen. I'm twenty-five.
CELIA: [*with a laugh*] God, sorry, Sheena. I figured you must like younger men.
SHEENA: Uh, no.
CELIA: Sorry. My mistake.

> SHEENA, *aware she's been rude, tries to sound cheerful.*

SHEENA: What time do you want us to start?
CELIA: Soon as there's enough light to see the fruit. Five okay? I'll honk the horn on the ute.

*Maeve Dermody (left) as Zoe and Anne Looby as Celia in the 2006
Griffin Theatre Company production in Sydney. (Photo: Robert McFarlane)*

SHEENA: Whatever. So… um… thanks. Goodnight.

>SHEENA *heads off to the shack.*

>ZOE *emerges from the house. She holds a drink full of ice cubes and rolls the icy glass across her face.*

CELIA: First stinking hot day really knocks you round.

ZOE: This is my new method to cool my brain down.

CELIA: Give us a go.

>ZOE *holds the glass to* CELIA*'s cheek.*

Yeah, that works. She's a prickly one. Sheena.

ZOE: Bit old for the guy, isn't she?

CELIA: Ah, see, we were both wrong. They're half-brother and sister.

ZOE: Oh. That fits.

CELIA: Hope I haven't made a mistake having them here.

ZOE: Why?

CELIA: Well, they seem sort of—

ZOE: What, you're into judging them already?

CELIA: No. No. Well, a bit maybe.

ZOE: More than a bit.

CELIA: It's a matter of trying to read people. Hope they'll be okay in that musty old shack.

>*She looks at* ZOE *staring down at the shack.*

What are you thinking about?

>ZOE *smiles and shrugs.*

Come and watch a bit of crap telly with me—for the fifteen minutes before I sink into a coma.

ZOE: Might muck around on the net for a while.

CELIA: Oh. Okay.

ZOE: See you at dawn.

>ZOE *and* CELIA *exit.*

♦ ♦ ♦ ♦ ♦

SCENE THREE

Outside the shack. Night.

KIERAN *flops onto the ground, exuberant about being exhausted.*

KIERAN: Finished! Our little cubby's cleaner and nicer than any place I've ever lived.

SHEENA *follows him outside.* KIERAN *leaps to his feet, hyper.*

Check out those peach trees—whap, whap, whap—all in rows. Growing food. What a top thing. I could do this. Grow stuff. What do you reckon it'd cost to buy a place like this?

SHEENA: Oh right, and where would you get the money?

KIERAN: I'm just saying, if you could, if you could, be awesome.

SHEENA: Kieran. Don't get carried away. We only just got you—

KIERAN: Yeah, I'm too useless to run a farm.

SHEENA: I'm not saying that.

KIERAN: What do you reckon about Zoe?

SHEENA: Bit up herself.

KIERAN: You reckon? I didn't think up herself. She's really—ah—what's the word…? [*He whacks at head to clear it.*] Wish my brain would work… Zoe seems really— Why won't my brain work?

SHEENA: Kieran. Go to bed. You and me are gonna work our guts out tomorrow. More peaches we pick, sooner we get the car back.

KIERAN: That's the plan. Thanks, Sheena. Have I said thanks?

SHEENA: About four thousand million times.

KIERAN: Yeah. Ha! But I mean it.

SHEENA: Sleep. Now.

KIERAN *salutes, then darts forward to squeeze her, laughing. Then he dashes inside, leaving* SHEENA *on her own.*

DOROTHY *appears in her dressing-gown and gumboots.*

DOROTHY: [*to the audience*] For some people, the sweet blessing of sleep comes easily.

SHEENA *is startled to see* DOROTHY *wandering about.* SHEENA *nods hello, trying to be polite.*

[*To* SHEENA] But some of us, we're awake half the night, churning things around in the mind.

SHEENA: Sorry?

DOROTHY: I'm muttering about myself like a mad, old chicken.

SHEENA: Oh.

SHEENA *waits for* DOROTHY *to leave.* DOROTHY *doesn't leave.*

DOROTHY: The boy—he's already asleep?

SHEENA: Kieran… oh, yeah. Deep asleep in thirty seconds. Like a baby.

DOROTHY: Ah, lucky. He's not kept awake with worries.

SHEENA: No way.

DOROTHY: He doesn't hold a thought in his head for very long.

SHEENA: Ten seconds tops.

DOROTHY: You have to do the thinking and worrying for him.

SHEENA: Yep. Lucky Sheena.

DOROTHY: He's impulsive. A little foolish sometimes.

SHEENA: A total bloody idiot sometimes.

DOROTHY: But no nasty bones in his body.

SHEENA: No. Compared to my other maggot brothers. Compared to me.

> *She feels* DOROTHY *looking at her, curious.*

We grew up in the same hopeless, joke house with the same custard-brained mother, but we got different fathers. Kieran's a good kid—not what he does, but in his heart. You don't see that in many people.

DOROTHY: So you don't want to see it get poisoned.

SHEENA: Which can happen to a guy like Kieran.

DOROTHY: He's got no protective coating.

SHEENA: He gets sucked in by the wrong people. Gets himself in a mess.

DOROTHY: In a mess?

> SHEENA *shrugs, clams up.*

SHEENA: He's got me to look out for him, now.

> DOROTHY *nods.* SHEENA*'s tone is sharp—the subject is closed.* SHEENA *makes a move to leave.*

Anyway—umm—I'd better—

DOROTHY: Some nights, you wish you could have amnesia—wipe the mind clean, forget the worries.

> SHEENA *shrugs, won't make eye contact.*

I'm talking about myself again.

> SHEENA *meets* DOROTHY*'s gaze, then quickly turns away.*

SHEENA: I better get to bed.

DOROTHY: Oh. Yes. Sleep well.

> SHEENA *exits quickly.*

[*To the audience*] When you're an old crone, you hardly don't sleep at all. So me—the Queen of the Night—I see the light come on up the hill in the smallest hours.

> CELIA *emerges from her house, yanking on a dressing-gown. When she sees* DOROTHY *they exchange a smile. This is a familiar night-time ritual for them.*

CELIA: I'm all right in the daytime, y'know.

DOROTHY: In daylight, your thoughts are busy with the thousand jobs that need doing.

CELIA: I know I'm an anxious person.

DOROTHY: But on the normal scale.

CELIA: Well, at the anxious end of normal.

DOROTHY: Okay.

> *They smile.*

CELIA: But two in the morning I wake up and—oh…

DOROTHY: The dangers are there.

CELIA: They ooze up while I'm asleep until my brain is awash with panic.

DOROTHY: Always about Zoe.

> CELIA *nods.*

CELIA: The world is a dangerous place. Most people have the luxury of ignoring that.

DOROTHY: But some of us don't.

CELIA: No. When Zoe was born, they put her on my chest and she looked me straight in the eye. The challenge was there. I must protect this person.

DOROTHY: But you never cotton-woolled Zoe.

CELIA: As an act of will. I never wanted to infect her with the fears.

DOROTHY: You let her run.

CELIA: I watched her climb trees and dive off highboards.

DOROTHY: But now she's older, it's more difficult.

CELIA: Now there's so much… At night, terrifying thoughts—toxic residue—it silts up in here.

DOROTHY: You repeat these thoughts over and over.

CELIA: A quarter of all road fatalities are in the fifteen- to twenty-year-old age group. Many girls contract human papilloma virus during their first sexual experience. Youth suicide—increased thirty-five per cent over the last ten years. The average age of first heroin use has dropped from twenty to sixteen.

DOROTHY: So many terrifying numbers.

CELIA: If I list them, meditate on them, they won't happen. I know that's crazy.

DOROTHY: Crazy, yes, but—

DOROTHY *shrugs—what can you do?*

CELIA: Night-worrying—it's the mother's voodoo. So in the daytime I can be normal and sturdy and get on with things.

DOROTHY *smiles, strokes* CELIA*'s head.*

DOROTHY: Try to a get couple of hours sleep now.

CELIA *heads back inside the house.*

[*To the audience*] This is the trade Celia has made. She spends the night in this dark place so in the day, she can face the world.

♦ ♦ ♦ ♦ ♦

SCENE FOUR

Feeble dawn light.

CELIA *is already briskly moving about, working.* KIERAN *bounds up from the shack.*

DOROTHY: [*to the audience*] Pickers start early—before the heat of the day—to get the peaches into the coolroom. Warm fruit doesn't handle or travel so good.

KIERAN: This is the absolute best time of the day, doncha reckon, Sheena? Magical.

SHEENA*, stumbling blearily behind him, is not convinced.*

I've stayed awake until dawn but I've never, like, approached it from this angle.

SHEENA: Kieran.

KIERAN *dutifully shuts up.* CELIA *brings out the picking gear.*

CELIA: Sorry about honking the horn. Bit brutal, I know.

ZOE enters. KIERAN *leaps across to her.*

KIERAN: Zoe. Hi.

ZOE: Hi.

KIERAN doesn't take his eyes off her. ZOE *is unnerved by his staring—but she likes it too.*

CELIA *tosses* KIERAN *and* SHEENA *some battered straw hats.*

CELIA: Gets blistering hot out there.

DOROTHY: So the more you pick in the cool of the day the better.

CELIA: A steady working pace is the go.

SHEENA: Hear that, Kieran? Steady working.

KIERAN: You watch me. I'm gonna be so good, you'll be going, 'Is that Kieran? It can't be! That sensible, hardworking legend of a guy can't be my basket-case little brother!'

ZOE smiles. She knows he's showing off for her.

CELIA: Okay. This week, we'll pick the Red Havens—this section here.

As CELIA explains, KIERAN *picks up the peaches, squints at the colours, sniffs them, brushes the furry skin against his cheek.* SHEENA *flashes him a warning look—you look weird.*

Start today with a colour pick—taking peaches coloured from this to, say, this— [*She holds up examples of fruit.*] After the colour pick, we do the strip pick: take off whatever fruit's left.

SHEENA, *noticing* KIERAN *is staring at* ZOE, *thumps him.*

Let's get cracking.

As DOROTHY talks to the audience, the light intensifies to the full glare of summer sun.

SHEENA *and* KIERAN *work picking peaches, emptying the picking bags into a bin.* CELIA *dashes to and from the shed, checking progress, giving hints and instructions.*

DOROTHY: [*to the audience*] Any fair person would say they were good workers. By the second day, they were bringing in the fruit at a decent rate. The boy—he was clowning around one minute, working fast like a crazy person the next minute. But added together, he picked the same amount as a good picker.

KIERAN *leaps about, hyperactive, trying to make* SHEENA *smile.*

SHEENA: Just get on with it.

KIERAN: Check out the face. Ouch. Who could ever make Mrs Crankypants smile?

SHEENA: Kieran. I said—

Something about his face makes her relent and she smiles.

KIERAN: Ah ha! Ha!

He dances triumphantly, juggling fruit. He hears ZOE *laugh and spins around to see her watching him.*

CELIA *comes down from the shed and chucks water bottles to* KIERAN *and* SHEENA. *They stop work to guzzle water.*

Thanks heaps for this.

CELIA: You need to keep the water up.

KIERAN: Reckon. Feel like my guts, my liver, my entire insides, have melted and sweated right out of me.

CELIA: You're going really well.

KIERAN: Yeah? Well, it's fun.

CELIA: So, Kieran, you would've finished school—what, last year, I guess.

KIERAN: Oh, well, not exactly.

CELIA: Did you leave early?

KIERAN: Kind of.

CELIA: You guys are exploring the country a bit, are you?

KIERAN: I guess. Is that what we're doing, Sheena?

CELIA: Is there a time frame? I mean, have you got plans for after—?

KIERAN: Oh, well… see, things got a bit messy and Sheena thought—

SHEENA: Shouldn't we get back to work?

KIERAN *smiles to* CELIA *and then throws himself back into work. As* CELIA *goes, she passes* ZOE.

CELIA: Hey, gorgeous.

ZOE: I'll do some picking, too.

CELIA: I need you in the shed.

ZOE: You and Dorothy can handle the packing. How else are we going to get the fruit in fast enough?

CELIA *watches* ZOE *head across to the pickers, then exits.*

Alice Parkinson as Sheena in the 2006 Griffin Theatre Company production in Sydney. (Photo: Robert McFarlane)

ZOE *starts picking. As* DOROTHY *speaks, we see* KIERAN *and* ZOE *talking, with* ZOE *growing in confidence.*

DOROTHY: [*to the audience*] Zoe was always a chatterbox—to me, to her Mum, to Sandor before he died. Every detail about what she did, what she saw, would come tumbling out of her mouth. Lately, not so chatty. She's on the internet or off with her own secret thoughts. But with this boy, by the end of the first week, it was yabber, yabber, yabber.

We tune in to ZOE *and* KIERAN*'s conversation:*

ZOE: The thing you have to know about me is that I'm socially retarded.

KIERAN: [*with a laugh*] What?

ZOE: Let me explain how it works. I go to a catholic girls' school way down near the border. A total of two and a half hours a day on a bus with a few old ladies going to the podiatrist to get their toenails scraped out. School, bus, home, weekends helping out round here. That's it. Goody-goody daughter, whether I like it or not. I live in protective custody.

KIERAN: Yeah? Your Mum seems—

ZOE: Mum believes in openness. I've always had lots of information about sex, drugs, whatever. She doesn't have to forbid me to do anything. I don't ask.

KIERAN: I don't get it.

ZOE: She does it by emotional blackmail. I can hear the worry clunking round in her brain even though she tries to hide it. What happened to my dad, that's—

KIERAN: That was such a terrible, rank thing. Your dad was just standing there, buying milk and—bang—some psycho shoots him.

ZOE: It's there in her mind: 'People go off in the morning and then never come home'. I missed the bus once and didn't phone. When I got home, she tried to sound reasonable, but I saw the panic on her face. I never want to see that face so I don't do anything. That's how she keeps me locked up in protective custody. That's how you end up a sixteen-year-old who's done fucking nothing. That is, you end up socially retarded.

KIERAN *is staring at her.*

What?

KIERAN *smiles then shakes his head.*

I talk too much. Sorry.

KIERAN: No, no. I like it. I don't get all the things you say but the bits I do get, I like a lot.

We see or hear CELIA *yell from the packing shed.*

CELIA: [*offstage, calling*] Zoe! Can you take over in the shed while I make some calls?

ZOE: Coming!

ZOE *runs off towards the shed.*

DOROTHY: [*to the audience*] By the end of the second week, Zoe developed some kind of hearing problem. She didn't hear Celia call her many of the times. So the talking went on. And—oh—the flirting went on.

ZOE *runs back down with food and sets it down in a shady spot.* KIERAN *hurls himself on the ground at* ZOE's *feet like an enthusiastic puppy.*

KIERAN: I've still got shocking pain in the guts.

SHEENA *finishes work and makes her way over to them.*

SHEENA: Your own stupid fault.

ZOE: How many peaches did you eat last night?

KIERAN: Ohhh, lost count after the first five or six. Chucked up one lot, ate some more.

KIERAN *and* ZOE *are attentive with each over the food—breaking pieces off and offering them, taking any excuse to touch each other's hands, etc.*

DOROTHY: [*to the audience*] It was sweet to see it. Even the sour one, the sister, loosened up a little.

SHEENA *sits near the other two as they all eat.*

ZOE: I still want to know how you guys ended up here.

SHEENA: This is where my car broke down.

ZOE: No, I mean, where you were going to?

KIERAN: We weren't going to anywhere. It was—

SHEENA *flashes him her fiercest warning look.*

Nah, I want to tell.

SHEENA: Kieran.

KIERAN: Sheena, Sheena, you gotta let me explain. To Zoe. Come on.

SHEENA: Tell her about what exactly?

KIERAN: About when you found me.

SHEENA: Just about that day? Okay.

KIERAN: Few months ago—

SHEENA: When I wasn't around. Tell her that.

KIERAN: Yeah, get this: Sheena moved up the Gold Coast. To be with this guy who—

SHEENA: Let's just say he turned out to be a dickless wonder.

KIERAN: Sheena picks the biggest dropkicks. She—

SHEENA *throws him a look—shut up.*

So. Sheena ended up back in Sydney.

SHEENA: First thing I asked Mum was, 'Where's Kieran?' She goes—

KIERAN: 'He's been staying at his mate Mick's place.'

SHEENA: 'Which Mick? Brain-dead Mick Fraser or Mick the toxic little scumbag?' And Mum fluttered her eyelids down.

KIERAN: [*demonstrating*] Like this.

SHEENA: Like she's too tired.

KIERAN: It's all too much for her.

SHEENA: Which it is.

KIERAN: Sheena gunned it round to Scumbag Mick's place.

SHEENA: I could smell the house from two doors down. So much blood in the living room, I thought someone had been killed there.

ZOE: What was the blood from?

SHEENA: Those geniuses got hold of industrial quantities of K.

ZOE: That's ketamine, isn't it? I read stuff on the net. Ketamine's actually a horse anaesthetic.

SHEENA: Yeah, well, if a human being overdoes it, binges, their feet and hands go numb. So they don't feel any pain. There was broken glass on the floor—

ZOE: Because—?

SHEENA: Accidents with bottles no one cleaned up. These morons didn't realise they were cutting their feet up.

ZOE: So they tracked blood all over.

SHEENA: The K wasn't what worried me.

KIERAN: Sheena thinks Mick is a dangerous guy.

SHEENA: A scaly, little toad and a psycho. The kind of genius who holds a shotgun to a mate's head as a joke.

KIERAN: That was only one time. Oh… well, twice but—

SHEENA: Mick'd gone into business for himself since I'd been away.

KIERAN: Dealing crystal.

SHEENA: He got Kieran frying his brains plus using him as a runner. Mick's in business with bikers.

KIERAN: Those guys are pretty big in the crystal business.

SHEENA: Mick was boasting to me how he's got a fucking shotgun in the house.

KIERAN: In case his business associates get unhappy about anything.

SHEENA: Don't have to be Mystic Sheena to see someone's gonna go to jail or end up dead. And chances are it's going to be my gullible little brother.

> KIERAN *strikes a pose for* ZOE *who laughs.*

I found Kieran in a corner.

KIERAN: Away with the pixies down a K-hole.

ZOE: So what did you do?

SHEENA: Dragged Kieran out the door, feet cut up to buggery. Shoved him in the back seat of my car.

KIERAN: Me too out of it to know what was going on.

SHEENA: Then I drove. As far away from Mick and Sydney as I could get. Kieran slept the first ten hours.

ZOE: But when he woke up, what did he—?

SHEENA: Started whining.

KIERAN: [*sending himself up*] 'My feet hurt—ow, ow ow!'

SHEENA: I bandaged up the cuts on his feet.

KIERAN: 'Where are you taking me? You're not the boss of me.'

ZOE: Why didn't you just run off?

KIERAN: I tried.

SHEENA: His feet were so cut up to begin with, he couldn't walk properly.

KIERAN: I was her prisoner in the back seat of the car. 'You're kidnapping me. This is an actual crime, y'know.'

SHEENA: Driving me mental.

KIERAN: So you know what she did? Pulled up outside a police station and she goes:

SHEENA: 'Okay then, pop inside and tell them I'm kidnapping you.'

> KIERAN *shrugs and grins to* ZOE—*what could he do?*

ZOE: But once your feet healed up, why didn't you take off then?

SHEENA: We'd been away from those deadheads long enough for Kieran to think straight. Now he needs to stay away from trouble long enough to grow a brain in his thick skull. [*Getting to her feet*] Lunchbreak's over. Back to work.

KIERAN: Gimme one more sec off my sore feet.

> SHEENA *goes back to picking.*

ZOE: Do you mind her bossing you around?

KIERAN: Oh, she doesn't always boss me around.

SHEENA: Kieran! You said one sec. Get over here! Now!

KIERAN: She looked after me even when I was in kindy. If some kid monstered me, Sheena'd belt across the playground like Super Sister and yank their arms behind their backs. It was like having my own bouncer. I don't know why she picked me—out of all us brothers. I mean… we were all clueless.

SHEENA: Kieran! No one's paying you to sit on your fucking arse!

KIERAN: She's a good person Sheena. She deserves better than she gets.

> ZOE *watches him carefully, even more smitten.*

> KIERAN *and* SHEENA *continue picking as the light fades to evening.*

DOROTHY: [*to the audience*] Hot days. Forty-one degrees. Not so bad for the peaches in the coolroom. But the people picking the peaches—no coolroom for them. Even in the evening, still sweltering hot.

> KIERAN *and* SHEENA *take off their picking bags as* ZOE *comes over with water bottles.* KIERAN *dribbles water over his face and head. He pulls at his aching shoulders, groans.*

SHEENA: I told you to take it easy with that high-up stuff.

KIERAN: I like it, though. I can locate all these muscles exactly—because they're aching. I can imagine my insides like one of those charts at the doctor's—y'know, with the man's skin taken off so you can see the red, stripy muscles wrapping and crossing over his body. How wild is that!

> ZOE *laughs.*

SHEENA: Shower. I'm not sleeping in that sauna of a shed with you all stinky and cheesy.

KIERAN: I love you too, Sheena. Might sleep out under the stars tonight.

SHEENA: Mozzies'd eat you alive.

KIERAN: Yeah? There goes that idea.

SHEENA: Well, you better—

KIERAN: Yeah, I'll be down in a sec.

> *Reluctantly* SHEENA *exits.*

ZOE: Sheena's shitty with you. Because of me.

KIERAN: She's worried that you're after me to steal all my money.

ZOE: And she's worried that you're immature and silly.

> KIERAN *and* ZOE *nod, mock grave, until* KIERAN *squirts her with water.* ZOE *squirts him back, laughing wildly, until they collapse onto their backs, breathless.*

KIERAN: What are you thinking this nano-second?

ZOE: About how I think about things too much. Like, in my imagination I watch myself doing something before I do it and then I don't end up doing anything. I wish I could just— [*closing her eyes, flinging her arms out expansively*] —blaagghh—throw myself into things before I even— You think I'm a fruit loop.

KIERAN: No, no, you're—uh—uh—uh—

ZOE: [*with a laugh*] Are you having a seizure?

KIERAN: I've gotta find exactly the right word. Ah! Yeah! You're spectacular.

ZOE: Shut up. You're taking the piss out of me.

KIERAN: Don't knock my word—I had to dig around in my scrambled brain to find that word. Spectacular.

ZOE: A spectacularly sad case, you mean.

KIERAN: Fuck me dead, you're beautiful.

> *That sucks the breath out of* ZOE *and she shuts up.* KIERAN *leans right over her but hesitates, waiting for permission. She reaches up to him and they kiss, tentative at first and then passionate.*

CELIA: Zoe! Where are you?

> ZOE *scrambles to her feet and runs off.*

SCENE FIVE

Bright sunlight.

KIERAN, SHEENA *and* ZOE *are picking.* CELIA *collects bins.*

As they work, KIERAN *and* ZOE *can't keep their hands off each other—kissing, laughing, whispering, in their own world.*

DOROTHY: [*to the audience*] I think we have a choice—how to look at it. 'Oh, those young lovers are too immature and foolish.' Or we can look with bitter eyes—'How dare those young people have such rapture'. I'm selfish. I feed off the energy that radiates out from their passion. I'm a geriatric vampire. When you have seen many bad things in a life, you yearn to see good things.

    CELIA *comes over to* SHEENA.

CELIA: Has Kieran had a serious girlfriend before now or—?

SHEENA: If you're trying to pump me for information, forget it. Kieran's not telling me anything you can't see with your own eyes.

CELIA: I'm just trying to get a sense of—

SHEENA: They're not fucking on Kieran's bed, if that's what you want to know.

CELIA: Fair enough, Sheena. I don't think it's so weird for me to be concerned about—

SHEENA: Hey. No offence to your daughter, but I'm not too stoked about this either, okay?

CELIA: Why do you say that?

SHEENA: Look, Kieran got himself in some trouble in Sydney so I'm—

CELIA: Trouble?

SHEENA: I'm just trying to keep him settled and this doesn't help.

    SHEENA *heads back to work.*

DOROTHY: [*yelling to someone offstage*] Are you here to check on me? I'm okay.

    JOE *enters and gives* DOROTHY *a kiss. She grabs his face to scrutinise it.*

Show me your eyeballs. You have a deficiency.

JOE: What is it this week, Mum? Vitamin B? E?

DOROTHY: A deficiency of the spirit.

> JOE *smiles, long-suffering. He shouts 'G'day' to* KIERAN, SHEENA *and* ZOE *as he walks over to* CELIA.

JOE: They seem to be moving through the pick okay.

CELIA: We're getting there.

> JOE *witnesses a burst of pashing between* KIERAN *and* ZOE.

JOE: Oh.

CELIA: Yeah.

> *The two of them watch for a moment.*

CELIA: Kieran's been in some kind of trouble.

JOE: Like what?

CELIA: The sister just said 'trouble'. That's why they're on the road. Kieran calls himself a 'fuck-up'. I know you'll think I'm neurotic, but I'm worried that—

JOE: Hey, no reason to panic. You don't know if he's—

CELIA: If he's in trouble with the police, would you be able to ask around and find out?

JOE: Well, in theory, yeah, but—

CELIA: Please, Joe. I've got nothing against this kid, but I've got them staying on the place.

JOE: I'm sorry if bringing them here was a mistake.

CELIA: No, you saved our skin last month, bringing them. I just need to know whether I should worry. Can you find out? Please.

JOE: Even if Kieran's been a bit wild, a lot of kids go through that. I mean, didn't you have some wild times?

CELIA: Exactly. It was only dumb luck I didn't die in a car with some drunk fuckwit.

JOE: And the reality is most kids don't die.

CELIA: But some do.

JOE: You can't worldproof her.

CELIA: Why can't I pick out a path for my child through the minefield if that means she—?

JOE: You can't limit the natural kind of—the natural sort of—

CELIA: You wouldn't let nature take its course if a wild dog leapt into a baby's cot.

JOE: No, but a small baby isn't the—

CELIA: Isn't the same as a sixteen-year-old. I know. But what if he drives her into a tree? What if he breaks her heart so utterly it's mangled forever? What if he drags her down into a world where—I don't know—a world where—

JOE's *mobile rings. He looks at the caller ID grimly.*

CELIA: Answer it. I'm just—I'm okay.

JOE: Sorry. Don't worry so much, Celia. See how things go. [*He walks away, talking on the phone.*] Fiona, hi. I'm— [*Pause.*] Yeah, sorry, the meeting this arvo took longer than— [*Pause.*] I said I'm sorry. [*Pause.*] On my way now.

DOROTHY *looks to the audience—see what I mean?* CELIA *signals goodbye to* JOE *as she exits.*

JOE *walks by* SHEENA.

Sheena. I spoke to the mechanic. The parts came, so your car's ready to pick up whenever—

SHEENA: When I get the money.

JOE: Sure. Right.

SHEENA *realises she sounded snappy and rude.*

SHEENA: Sorry. Sorry… I'm just—

JOE: You've got a lot to worry about.

SHEENA: Yeah.

JOE: Give me a yell if you guys need anything.

SHEENA: You're being so nice to us. That's your job in town, isn't it?— being the nice, helpful guy.

JOE: Eh?

SHEENA: Oh, I'm not having a go at you. I'm saying it's a good thing. Decent.

JOE: Oh, well… I don't know if—

SHEENA: I'm just saying I reckon— Look, y'know, thanks.

KIERAN *and* ZOE *have a parting kiss before* SHEENA *drags* KIERAN *off.* JOE *goes to leave.* ZOE *steps in his path.*

ZOE: What were you talking to Mum about? I saw her doing the worried face.

JOE: Yeah, well, she's—

ZOE: She thinks I can't see it. But I've been copping that face all day.

JOE: Go easy on her.

ZOE: Come on, you must know what it's like. You've got a crazy paranoid mother, too.

JOE: Your mother's not crazy, Zoe. I don't know how much she talks to you about the past.

ZOE: I do think about what happened to Mum. I'm not heartless.

JOE: I know you're not.

ZOE: But it's a bit unreal, y'know. I've got photos of my dad and I try to imagine stuff, but…

JOE: My mother and father never talked much about the war and '56 and after. But there'd be odd mentions—people who died, went missing. I kept a mental tally, adding up all the dead people in my head. I think—when your parents have huge loss like that—you grow up with an extra burden. Extra pressure to stay alive.

ZOE: And stay happy. I can't even let on if I'm feeling down, in case she gets panicky.

JOE: [*smiling*] Yeah. But they still know. You can't fool them.

ZOE: You think I should let her lock me away.

JOE: No. Just understand where it comes from.

ZOE: I can't let that decide everything.

JOE: Well… maybe that's right.

He squeezes her in an affectionate hug.

Take care, Zoe.

JOE *exits.*

CELIA *enters and watches* ZOE *tip her head back and let water from a bottle run through her hair and down her singlet. She inhales deeply, stretching her limbs with achy pleasure.* CELIA *watches* ZOE.

ZOE: I know you're there.

CELIA: I was thinking how beautiful you are.

ZOE: You want to reach into my head and check out every thought that's in here.

CELIA: You used to tell me every thought. But I know that time's over.

ZOE: Yeah?

CELIA: I just want you to be careful. You know so little about Kieran and maybe you should—

ZOE: You don't understand.

CELIA: It's exciting. This is the first time you've really liked a guy.

ZOE: 'Liked'.

CELIA: Okay, more than like. I'm saying I understand you're giddy with this and—

ZOE: No. You don't want to understand.

CELIA: Of course I want to understand. Why would you say that?

ZOE: I can see the way you're setting your jaw, that warnings will come out of your mouth and 'what ifs' and 'always remember'.

CELIA: But can't I—?

ZOE: No. Shut your mouth. I won't listen to you pour your poison on this.

> ZOE *walks off and* CELIA *retreats inside.*

♦ ♦ ♦ ♦ ♦

SCENE SIX

Night.

KIERAN *emerges from the shack, towelling his hair dry.* ZOE *comes running out of the orchard, breathless.*

KIERAN: What's up? You okay?

ZOE: I was thinking.

KIERAN: Yeah?

ZOE: That we should have sex now.

KIERAN: Oh. Right. If you want to. I mean, yes yes… y'know, great. That'd be great.

ZOE: But then I was thinking, what are my reasons? Would I just be using Kieran?

> *He laughs and reaches for her.*

KIERAN: You can use me. That's cool. Use me.

> *She pulls away, yabbering.*

ZOE: I mean, would I just be fucking you to rile up my mother? Or for the sake of getting rid of it? I've never understood why people say 'losing virginity'. What are you losing? The absence of something. Which is nothing. Really you're gaining non-virginity. You're gaining sexual experience. Which in a way is—

KIERAN: Zoe.

ZOE: Sorry. I'm raving on.

KIERAN: Which is cool. I just don't know—

ZOE: Nervous. Sorry. But it's complicated. I want to be sure what my reasons are. Sorry.

KIERAN: I'm not sure what you want me to do. We can keep talking if you—

ZOE: No. No.

> KIERAN *pulls her close and kisses her. He starts to unbutton her clothes.*

Your hands are shaking.

KIERAN: [*looking at his hands*] Oh. Yeah.

ZOE: Why should you be nervous? You've done this before.

KIERAN: Never when I wasn't off my face on something.

ZOE: Which is different, I guess.

KIERAN: Yes.

> *He stops for a moment, dropping his head on her shoulder.*

And I've never done this with you.

ZOE: And what, that makes you nervous because—?

KIERAN: Doesn't make me nervous. It amazes me.

> ZOE *grabs him, kissing him hungrily. Then she starts yanking at his jeans with mock desperation, making* KIERAN *laugh. She drags him into the orchard, offstage.*

DOROTHY: [*to the audience*] Sometimes—if you make yourself still and quiet—you can tap into things that are going on in the world of people. Like tuning in to an underground radio station. Listening to the powerful moments from a thousand years ago, fifty years ago, or happening right now somewhere. For example, a moment of passion happening as I am speaking to you now.

> SHEENA *comes out of the shack just as* KIERAN *wanders back, dreamy, euphoric.*

KIERAN: From over there, you can get a big lungful of warm peaches and it's—ah…

> KIERAN *inhales deeply and staggers, mock stoned.*

SHEENA: Kieran, we need to—

KIERAN: I've been thinking—I could get a job on a farm growing stuff. That's something I could do, I reckon.

SHEENA: We could follow the picking circuit if you like. Grapes in Mildura, then head along the Murray in time for the tomatoes.

KIERAN: Why leave here? There's plenty of work. We could finish the peaches, then the apricots.

SHEENA: The mother's sniffing around, asking questions.

KIERAN: She'll be right. Celia's a bit freaked out, sure. You know what happened to Zoe's dad. I mean, that poor lady. That's why she gets worried.

SHEENA: I'm worried. This little girl's using you.

KIERAN: What?

SHEENA: I watched that girl from the first day we got here. She's out to get her thrills and give mummy the shits and have something to boast about to her little princess friends at school. 'What I did in my summer holidays: I fucked a wild, trashy boy from Sydney.'

KIERAN: That is not true.

SHEENA: It's gonna end up bringing big trouble for you. And when she's had enough of her little adventure, that girl won't give a toss what happens to you.

KIERAN: Sheena, don't talk like that, okay.

SHEENA: You've gotta trust me on this. The sooner we get away from here—

ZOE: [*whispering from the orchard*] Kieran. Kieran.

> ZOE *holds up an armful of blankets.* KIERAN*'s face lights up the instant he sees her.*

SHEENA: Kieran—

KIERAN: I don't want to fight with you, okay Sheena, and I know you're looking out for me and everything, but… y'know…

> KIERAN *runs off with* ZOE *into the orchard.*

DOROTHY: [*to the audience*] There were three clear nights in a row.

> KIERAN *and* ZOE *appear out of the orchard, wrapped in blankets. They flop down on the ground together.*

KIERAN: You're so lucky to live here. I like that if you felt like a feed, you'd just reach up and grab something.

ZOE: It's not always like this, you idiot. Only for three months.

KIERAN: Sure, sure—

ZOE: Half the year it's just grey sticks.

KIERAN: But you know that inside the grey stick trees there's little tiny peaches waiting to come out. [*He flops flat on his back, staring at the sky.*] I've been off my face a fair whack of the time since I was thirteen. Since I've been out on the road with Sheena, it's like I'm waking up and seeing things for the first time. It's like—oh, I want to explain this to you. I've been replaying stuff in my head.

ZOE: Like what?

KIERAN: Dumb stuff I did like going to a meeting with bikers, off my face, knowing Mick had a shotgun in the boot. It didn't rattle me then, but now I'm scared shitless. It's like now I'm feeling the fear I should have had then. My brain's catching up with what my body's been doing. Crazy, eh? All out of sync.

ZOE: Maybe you were out of sync before. But not now.

KIERAN: But the trouble is, trouble is—

> KIERAN *jumps to his feet, suddenly hyper.*

ZOE: [*with a laugh*] Sit down. What are you doing?

Scott Timmins as Kieran and Maeve Dermody as Zoe in the 2006 Griffin Theatre Company production in Sydney. (Photo: Robert McFarlane)

KIERAN: Just let me say this, okay.

ZOE: What?

KIERAN: You know I got in trouble with the cops when I was younger.

ZOE: Yeah.

KIERAN: Well, there's been some other stuff in the last few months. Then I didn't show up in court and that means I'm in deeper trouble.

> ZOE *grabs at his hand, trying to make him stay still.*

ZOE: I don't care. I trust you, Kieran, whatever happens.

KIERAN: But I don't trust myself. Sometimes I only see what's in front of me. A mate'll say, 'Let's do this or that, Kieran', and I think, 'Why not?', and I forget the important things and I mess up and—

> *She grabs his hand.*

ZOE: I'm right here.

KIERAN: You are. Why would you want me? I mean, I'm just—

> *She pulls him back down to her.*

ZOE: You're the most alive person I ever met.

◆ ◆ ◆ ◆ ◆

SCENE SEVEN

Day. The sound of heavy rain.

CELIA *dashes around the yard, pulling gear undercover.*

DOROTHY: [*to the audience*] We had twenty-four hours of heavy rain. No good for picking—because of risk that the fruit takes in too much water and the skins will split.

> JOE *enters.*

CELIA: Come in the house, out of the rain.

JOE: No, I kinda like being out in this. I spend most of my waking hours in offices.

CELIA: Dorothy's not here. We won't be packing any fruit on a day like this.

JOE: I came to see you.

CELIA: Oh.

JOE: I talked to a bloke I know in Sydney. A cop.

CELIA: Oh… Did he know anything about—?

JOE: Kieran was in some trouble as a juvenile.

CELIA: He's legally an adult now, though.

JOE: That's right. There are a couple of warrants out on him.

CELIA: Warrants for what?

JOE: Minor stuff mostly. A break-and-enter. Story is he got caught up with some nasty characters and police want to talk to him about a couple of things.

CELIA: Oh my God, Joe… what should I—?

JOE: The wisest thing is for them to move on. You could ask them to leave now rather than stay for the rest of the pick.

CELIA: Zoe talks about travelling with them when they move on.

JOE: Well, tell her she can't.

CELIA: She wouldn't listen. And she'd hate me for it.

JOE: Kieran seems like a good-hearted kid. Obviously Sheena's trying to straighten him out.

CELIA: Listen, I don't want to hurt this boy. All I'm thinking about is Zoe. I don't know what I should do.

> ZOE *enters, noticing* CELIA *and* JOE *talking.*

JOE: Talk to her. That's the best thing. Talk to Zoe.

> JOE *exits.* ZOE *walks up to where* CELIA *waits.*

ZOE: What were you talking to Joe about?

CELIA: I have to ask Kieran to leave.

ZOE: I knew it. I knew you'd end up—

CELIA: He's wanted by the police.

ZOE: I know. He told me.

CELIA: Wanted for robbery. Serious stuff. Did he tell you that?

> ZOE *is thrown for a second, then rallies.*

ZOE: Yes. He told me. Because he trusts me and I trust him. Which you wouldn't know any fucking thing about. Since you don't trust me one tiny—

CELIA: I do trust you.

ZOE: Bullshit. Did you sick Joe onto Kieran? To spy on him. That's disgusting. No, actually, it's sad. Is your life so dried-up and gutless that you have to snuffle around in the dirt 'til you find a way to destroy what other people—?

CELIA: You can say as many cruel things to me as you like, Zoe. I have to do what I think is right.

ZOE: You really don't want me to have anything, do you?

CELIA: No... Zoe sweetheart, you're wrong. It's because I want you to have everything—

ZOE: If you make Kieran leave, I'll go with him.

CELIA: Please... if you need to have a battle of wills with me, don't do it about this.

ZOE: You don't get it. It's not about you. I love Kieran.

CELIA: Zoe, you're sixteen.

ZOE: Kieran sees me. I can be my whole self with him with no editing bits out or worrying that bits of me cause him pain. I didn't know a person could feel a connection this strong and still bear it. Feels like I can go out there and take on anything. What I couldn't bear is being apart from Kieran.

ZOE stares at CELIA *challengingly, then walks off.*

DOROTHY: [*to the audience*] The rain dried up by the afternoon. But when I walked to the house—to see if we would start picking again, Celia wasn't there. Later, I saw her car come back from town.

♦ ♦ ♦ ♦ ♦

SCENE EIGHT

Night.

SHEENA *is outside the shack.* CELIA *approaches. She's shaky but determined.*

CELIA: Sheena.

SHEENA: Do you want help with those crates? I'm not sure where Kieran is but—

CELIA: I want to do a deal with you. I want you and Kieran to move on.

SHEENA: That's what I want. Soon as I get enough money together.

CELIA: I paid the bill at the mechanic's. I've asked Joe to drive the car out here tonight. I withdrew the cash I had in the bank. Two thousand six hundred. It's yours. Travelling money.

She hands SHEENA *an envelope of cash.*

I want you and Kieran to leave tonight, without Zoe knowing about it.

SHEENA: Kieran won't go for that idea.

CELIA: You should know that I know about Kieran's police trouble.

SHEENA: Oh. Right. So you'll go to the cops if we don't—

CELIA: I'm not threatening you.

SHEENA: Yeah, you are.

CELIA: Well, I don't want to make threats. I'm just trying to— Look, you want to stop this before it gets out of hand?

SHEENA: Yes.

CELIA: So do I. This is a solution that suits both of us.

CELIA *waits while* SHEENA *looks at the money in her hand.*

SHEENA: Fair enough.

CELIA: Thank you. Make sure Zoe doesn't know about this. Please.

SHEENA: She's going to wonder what the hell—

CELIA: I'll work that out. Once he's gone.

SHEENA *nods.* CELIA *exits, back to the house.*

SHEENA *looks at the money, then shoves it in her pocket.*

KIERAN *enters. He's hyper, bouncy.*

KIERAN: Sheena! Zoe showed me this swimming hole at the river! You gotta check it out later! Swimming in the rain—it was so—

SHEENA: Pack your stuff. We're leaving.

KIERAN: What? Why?

SHEENA: Celia knows about the Sydney stuff. She'll dob you in to the police if we don't clear off. We leave as soon as the car gets here.

KIERAN: What are you talking about?

SHEENA: She's given us a wad of money. The deal I made with Celia is we go tonight.

KIERAN: No. Hang on. I gotta talk to Zoe.

SHEENA: That's the other part of the deal. You can't tell Zoe.

KIERAN: No way, no way, no way—

SHEENA: There's no choice.

KIERAN: Wait, wait. Let me think a second. Let me think.

SHEENA: Plenty of time to think once we're in the car. I reckon this is the best thing.

KIERAN: It's not the best thing for me! Fuck!

KIERAN *is circling, agitated, muttering to himself.*

SHEENA: What makes you think you're a good thing for this girl? The way you are. Wake up. No wonder her mother wants you gone.

KIERAN: Why would you say that to me?

SHEENA: I'm sorry. But I've gotta look out for you.

KIERAN: Listen, listen—

SHEENA: What if Celia goes to the cops? Do you want to get done for the vet lab thing?

KIERAN: No.

SHEENA: Do you want to go to jail?

KIERAN: No, no.

SHEENA: So we have to go.

KIERAN *winds up into a panic, cursing to himself.*

KIERAN: Listen to me. I can't leave without seeing Zoe.

SHEENA: I'm the one who has to look at things realistically. We have to—

KIERAN: You're not listening to me. I love Zoe.

SHEENA: I know you think that. I know—

KIERAN: You don't know. You don't. When I'm with Zoe, things are so clear in my head. It's not all a screeching, tangled mess in here. And I think, 'Right, Kieran, this is what it should feel like'. And when Zoe looks at me, it's amazing—she doesn't see some hopeless case. When Zoe looks at me I feel like I could do anything in the universe. Are you listening to me?

SHEENA: Yes.

KIERAN: Please, Sheena.

SHEENA: What if I said you've got 'til midnight? But then we stick to the deal. You don't want to go to jail, do you? And you don't want to get Zoe in big trouble, do you?

KIERAN: No.

SHEENA: So you can't tell her we're going. Tell me you understand that.

KIERAN: I understand that.

SHEENA: Okay. Midnight—be back here and we go.

KIERAN *goes off.*

SHEENA *slumps for a moment, exhausted. Then she drags herself up and starts hauling stuff out of the shack, ready to go.*

JOE *enters.*

JOE: I left your car down by the gate.

SHEENA: How will you get back into town?

JOE: I'll stay the night at Mum's. Wouldn't mind to escape for a night. Where's Kieran?

SHEENA: He goes off in a sook when he has to do something he doesn't want to do.

JOE: You explained to him—

SHEENA: Kieran knows he doesn't have any choice, unless he wants to get arrested.

JOE: You know, Sheena, you made things harder for him by skipping town.

SHEENA: By the time I found him, he'd already missed those court dates.

JOE: The cops want to question him about some other matters.

SHEENA: Those morons broke into a vet science lab. Stole a shitload of ketamine. A security guard got bashed.

JOE: Do you know if Kieran was part of it?

SHEENA: He was there. Trailing after Mick like a brain-damaged puppy. With Kieran's record, he'd end up in jail for a serious deal like that, wouldn't he?

> JOE *shrugs, nods.*

Jail for a soft kid like Kieran.

JOE: Yeah. I know.

SHEENA: He needed rescuing. I rescued him.

JOE: What will you do now?

SHEENA: Go back to what we were doing before: driving round the west—figure eights on the map.

JOE: But in the long run...

SHEENA: I guess keep Kieran alive and out of major trouble. That's all I can do.

JOE: Well, good luck.

SHEENA: Deep down I always thought Kieran was doomed. But the last few weeks, he's been so grounded, really got into the work, he's—I dunno...

JOE: I don't think he's doomed.

SHEENA: Ohh... he's gonna hate my guts for making him leave. The next few weeks will be shitful. Kieran miserable, blaming me.

She starts to cry. JOE *fumbles to get out a hanky for her.*

Ta. You're a kind man, you know.

JOE: You reckon? Not so sure about that.

SHEENA: At least you think about what's going on for other people.

JOE: For all the good that does.

SHEENA: It's more than most people do. Kieran thinks the best of everyone so they take advantage of him. He doesn't know what people
are really after.

JOE: But you do?

SHEENA: Yeah. [*Laughing*] They still end up taking advantage of me,
but. Y'know, I've been a bit jealous—watching him and Zoe. Even
if they are kidding themselves. I wouldn't mind kidding myself like
that for a little while.

JOE*'s mobile phone rings.*

JOE: Sorry.

He looks at the caller ID, then switches off the phone. He feels
SHEENA *looking at him and smiles, shaking his head.*

SHEENA: What?

*Alice Parkinson as Sheena and John Adam as Joe in the 2006 Griffin
Theatre Company production in Sydney. (Photo: Robert McFarlane)*

JOE: The way you look at me—like you can read what's going on in my mind.

SHEENA: I can't really. It's just a thing I do with my face to make it seem like I've sussed people.

She exaggerates a suspicious gimlet stare.

JOE: [*laughing*] Well, it works.

SHEENA: Yeah, freaks people out, so they blurt stuff out without me doing anything.

JOE: I was just thinking… I guess I'm unnerved by the idea that—I've got people I have to worry about, responsibilities, history I have to remember. You get used to censoring yourself, talking yourself out of impulses. After a while, you lose connection with something inside. I can't explain it—sorry.

SHEENA: No, I think I get you.

JOE looks at SHEENA, hoping she understands. Then suddenly he slides closer and they kiss. When they stop kissing, JOE turns away a little.

Now you're thinking, this is a mistake, this'll cause problems. I mean, you're right, we probably shouldn't—

JOE: I'm thinking how incredibly soft your mouth is.

SHEENA: Oh.

They kiss again, more passionately.

I've got two beers left inside. Do you want one?

JOE: Yeah.

SHEENA and JOE exit, going into the shack.

◆ ◆ ◆ ◆ ◆

SCENE NINE

Night.

DOROTHY *appears in her nightie.*

DOROTHY: [*to the audience*] On the radio, the forecast for the next day was forty-two degrees. Heavy rain, then hot temperatures— you know what can happen? The fruit cooks on the trees. True. I wouldn't believe if I never saw it one year. I made up the spare bed for Joe, but Joe never showed up.

> *A torch beam cuts through the darkness. It is* CELIA *running around the yard with a torch.*

CELIA: Zoe! Zoe! Are you out here?

DOROTHY: [*to the audience*] I saw a car pass by my house just before midnight.

> CELIA *runs towards the shack with the torch, calling* ZOE.

> SHEENA *emerges, wrapping a sheet around herself.*

CELIA: Is Zoe down here?

SHEENA: No, I thought she was—

> CELIA *hears another person inside the shack.*

CELIA: Kieran? Kieran! Do you know where Zoe is?

> *But it is* JOE *who appears, hastily doing up his jeans.* CELIA *stops, taking this in.* SHEENA *runs past her into the darkness.*

JOE: Celia…

CELIA: Do you know where Kieran is?

JOE: Sheena thought he was cooling off and he'd be back.

CELIA: You don't know where he is?

JOE: No, we should've, uh… I'm sorry.

> CELIA *turns away from* JOE *and resumes calling out, sweeping the torch through the yard and orchard.*

CELIA: [*calling*] Zoe! Zoe!

> *The torch beam picks up* SHEENA*'s face.*

SHEENA: My car's gone.

> CELIA *is frozen for a moment.*

JOE: It'll be fine. We can—

CELIA: I'll find her. I'll find her.

> CELIA *runs into the darkness with the torch.*

END OF ACT ONE

ACT TWO

DOROTHY *enters, rugged up in warm clothes.*

DOROTHY: [*to the audience*] One thing I never liked about Australia is the seasons. In summer, grey-green leaves and grey-brown grass. Winter, the grey-green leaves still stuck there on the trees. You don't call that a season. The year has got no rhythm to swing a person through. But here around the orchards, the trees are bare, so it looks like winter.

After Sandor died, I had one consoling idea in my head: now, apart from Josef of course, I have just me to worry about. I can suit to myself. Eat sardines and chocolate mousse every night if I want. But I am going to be honest to you here—I did not eat many mousse. I drank vodka. Because the consoling idea was not so consoling. The vodka did a better job.

It was a couple of seasons after Sandor died when Celia said, 'Dorothy, I need help with packing the fruit'. I knew this is a plan that Celia and Josef cooked up to get me out and busy. But it happens that I am bloody good at it. So the year goes like this: Summer and autumn, I am up at five to work for Celia. Sober. Winter, back to my little underworld, with vodka and silly television shows to keep me company. There was a kind of swing and rhythm to the year. This winter is different. As you can see: sober. I have to be because there are people who need an eye kept onto them.

JOE *enters and comes over to give* DOROTHY *a kiss.*

JOE: Thought you might be prowling around up here. I dropped off some bags on your back porch.

DOROTHY: What bags? Bags of what?

JOE: We're sorting through stuff in the house. There were some things Fiona thought you might be able to use.

DOROTHY: Are these 'things' items of over-priced, foolish junk Fiona bought and now throws out so she can buy new?

JOE: Basically, yes.

DOROTHY: Will they be useful to me?

JOE: No. Except as a physical reminder of your contempt for Fiona.

DOROTHY: Then drop the bags at the Salvation Army in town, will you?

> JOE *nods.* DOROTHY *scrutinises him carefully.*

Josef. What's going on?

JOE: About what?

DOROTHY: You tell me about what.

JOE: Fiona asked me to move out.

DOROTHY: Ah. Is this for permanent?

JOE: Yes, it's permanent.

DOROTHY: You didn't have to confess to the sex.

> JOE *looks at her—he did have to.*

It's only that one intercourse—months ago, we're talking about. Isn't it?

JOE: Yes.

DOROTHY: The woman, Sheena—she wouldn't have told. Celia was gone away. I would never tell. So why—?

JOE: I felt I had no choice.

DOROTHY: So you confess and Fiona marches you to the counselling every week for three months. Now suddenly she decides to throw you out like the garbage?

JOE: The decision was mutual in many ways.

DOROTHY: I always knew this is what she will do in the end.

JOE: As you made very clear.

DOROTHY: But she wanted her months of watching you writhe with the guilt first.

JOE: Mum—

DOROTHY: I keep my mouth shut. Where will you live?

JOE: At the pub until I find somewhere.

DOROTHY: You are always welcome to live with me. Or you could travel, now that you're a single man again. Have some fun.

> *He looks at her pointedly.*

You don't want to be far from the children.

JOE: Of course I don't.

> JOE *walks over to look at the orchard.*

DOROTHY: [*to the audience*] There are men who can live apart from their children with no great suffering. Josef is not one of them. Do I wish he didn't love his children so much? Sometimes. It's strange to find yourself wishing that your child was a less deep feeling man, more petty and selfish. But you don't like to see something tearing at his insides.

JOE: The orchard's a mess.

DOROTHY: Of course. More than three months abandoned.

JOE: It's a problem if the trees are left overgrown for this long, isn't it?

DOROTHY: This is why the ginger-haired boy and his cousin should come and do the urgent work.

JOE: I could organise that for Celia.

DOROTHY: [*shaking her head*] I suggested this.

JOE: She can't think about anything.

DOROTHY: No.

> DOROTHY *grabs* JOE's *face to scrutinise him.*

JOE: Mum. Please. Don't.

DOROTHY: You're not eating. Stay for dinner.

JOE: I can't. I have to pick up Hamish from soccer.

DOROTHY: Ah. Of course. Well, let me parcel up some food for you to take back to your sad, little hotel room of shame.

JOE: Oh no, I'll—uh—okay. Thanks, Mum, that'd be lovely.

> JOE *exits, leaving* DOROTHY *to address the audience as the light fades to night.*

DOROTHY: [*to the audience*] The night Zoe ran away with the boy, Celia drove off looking for them. Oh—I should tell you that the sister gave back the money in the envelope. No one would say she was a charming girl, but she was a person of honour. So now Celia is gone, searching for her daughter. The rest of the peaches she has left to rot. A few times Zoe has sent Celia an email—'Don't worry'. Nothing else. Every day Celia rings me up. 'Has Zoe come home?' Every day, it breaks my heart. No. I have to say no. When I hang up the phone, she is still here. [*Indicating her own head*] Sometimes, it's like tuning in to a radio station I cannot bear. Where you must hear the childless mother's cry tear through the night.

◆ ◆ ◆ ◆ ◆

SCENE TWO

Night.

CELIA *appears out of the darkness. She and* DOROTHY *speak directly to the audience.*

CELIA: Every day I wake up in yet another motel room and for a few seconds I'm disoriented. Then the shock of it hits me fresh: my daughter is missing. But the world goes on.

DOROTHY: As if the universe is—unbelievably—not toxic and dead.

CELIA: My body continues to operate—blood and nerves and complex chemicals hum along…

DOROTHY: As if nothing has changed.

CELIA: When I started searching, I had plans, leads. Towns where Zoe knew someone or towns with backpacker hostels and picking work.

DOROTHY: Nothing.

CELIA: I left photos with people, I followed up any sighting of them or the car.

DOROTHY: Nothing.

CELIA: All logic has leaked out of my searching. I wander shopping centres and railway stations for eighteen hours a day, hoping I'll see her walk past. Yesterday I heard a woman screeching and I realised that woman was me.

DOROTHY: Screaming at strangers in the street.

CELIA: How dare they smile and drink coffee and go about their lives as if my daughter wasn't missing. When Paul, my husband, was killed, my first impulse was—I'll kill myself. But I was pregnant with Zoe. I remember being angry—that an escape route had been closed to me.

DOROTHY: Once you have a child, that option is annulled.

CELIA: Missing my husband… the pain would hit me in waves, knocking me off my feet.

DOROTHY: You can never predict when.

CELIA: But at the same time there was Zoe, this little creature who needed things—practical things—right now. And brought me such joy.

DOROTHY: It's astonishing the way two such strong feelings can exist inside your body at the same time.

CELIA: I try to save my energy for the night, when I really have to concentrate.

DOROTHY: Because night-time is when bad things happen to people.

CELIA: Wherever Zoe is.

> CELIA *and* DOROTHY *remain onstage as light comes up on:*
>
> *A carpark.* KIERAN *and* ZOE *enter, breathless, laughing, gulping for air from running.*

ZOE: Feel my heart. Feel my heart.

> *She presses* KIERAN*'s hand against her chest.*

Pounding like it's going to explode.

> *They laugh, getting their breath back. They break open a packet of jelly dinosaurs and chomp on them.*

KIERAN: You hurt yourself going over the fence?

ZOE: No—oh, a bit. Scratch from the barbed wire on the top.

> KIERAN *kisses her leg where she scratched it.*

KIERAN: Lucky that security guard was a pudgy, old guy or we'd be rooted.

ZOE: He didn't see us come into the carpark.

KIERAN: Nuh. We're sweet.

ZOE: [*with a laugh*] I can't believe you did that!

KIERAN: You wanted jelly dinosaurs.

ZOE: Yeah, but I didn't think you'd run in and grab them.

KIERAN: No money. I left that ten bucks back at Mick's.

ZOE: They taste better this way.

> *They chomp more dinosaurs.*

Whoo—the ground's moving—like I'm on a boat.

KIERAN: That's the not sleeping.

ZOE: How long have we been awake this time?

KIERAN: It must be—yeah, three days. Awake three days.

ZOE: Sorry if I was a bit weird before, at the house.

KIERAN: You don't wanna worry about the shit Mick goes on with. He comes across like a scary guy and his girlfriend—

ZOE: Jade. I feel sorry for her.

KIERAN: Me too. Poor old Jade. But Mick's all noise. He'd never do anything.

ZOE: That older guy—with the dead-fish eyes—

KIERAN: Yeah, his brain rotted in his skull years ago. You're a fast runner. And a good climber. Couldn't believe how you went over that fence like a monkey. Hey—what's wrong?

ZOE is suddenly panicky and whoosy.

ZOE: I'm seasick... no, dizzy—the ground's falling away under me.

KIERAN grabs her and eases her down to ground.

KIERAN: It's okay... the ground, see? Solid.

ZOE: I feel really weird. I feel really weird.

KIERAN: Reckon we need to sleep. Awake too many days in a row. It can do your head in. Mick and the guys in that house—that's how they live. Everything gets out of whack. Oh, shit... you look white, you're shaking.

ZOE: Let's fuck.

She leads KIERAN offstage.

Over here—there's some grass. Let's fuck right now.

They exit.

DOROTHY and CELIA, speaking directly to the audience.

CELIA: Every day I wake up around midday to ring the police and hospitals.

DOROTHY: Then to wait by the phone through the night.

CELIA: I couldn't bear the idea that I was sunk into mindless sleep, at the exact moment that Zoe was facing some monster.

DOROTHY: Sheena, she phoned here, out of some blue. 'Have you seen my brother?'

SHEENA appears.

SHEENA: I cut dead any feelings for Kieran. The night he buggered off. 'That's it. I can't care what happens to him anymore. I just want the car back.'

DOROTHY: You must try to get on with your own life.

SHEENA: I went back up the Gold Coast. The Dickless Wonder wasn't with anyone else—who'd have him?—so we ended up back together. Well, that idea turned out to be pretty ordinary. Normally, I could've used Kieran as the excuse to break it off with the Wonder but not this time—seeing as I don't care about Kieran anymore.

DOROTHY: Sometimes you have to make a decision for your own sake.

SHEENA: I announced to the guy, 'You're a Dickless Wonder and I'm leaving'. Ended up staying on the Gold Coast. It's ugly as sin and full of arseholes, but there's work. Streets full of people day or night.

DOROTHY: So there's always noise you can disappear into.

SHEENA: One time I saw some girl stumbling through the traffic with a bellyful of Bacardi Breezers. Looked a bit like Zoe. Another time I saw a kid who walked exactly like Kieran. But fuck it. I can't let myself wonder where he is.

DOROTHY: Or else you're up all night.

CELIA: All night, I conjure up images of what might be happening to her and run through the scenes of danger in my head.

DOROTHY: As if such vigilance is crucial.

CELIA: I summon up images of danger, examine them.

DOROTHY: As if that creates a kind of force-field around her.

CELIA: I know this is not logical. But somewhere deep in the animal guts of me, I believe that my dark chanting will be some protection for my child.

> DOROTHY, CELIA *and* SHEENA *remain onstage as lights come up on:*
>
> *Night.* ZOE *and* KIERAN *are asleep on the ground.*
>
> ZOE *jerks awake, panicky.* KIERAN *sleepily reaches out to comfort her.*

KIERAN: Hey… hey… Bad dream again?

> ZOE *nods.* KIERAN *hugs her close.*

You're shaking. Tell me the dream. Get it out of your head and gone.

ZOE: Oh… I don't know…

KIERAN: Where were you in the dream?

ZOE: I was walking through an underground carpark. The people wandering around—I knew they were dead… the way you can just know stuff in a dream?

KIERAN: I get you.

ZOE: I recognised faces. Sandor, this kid from primary school who died, my father. I always had photos of my father in my mind, but I never imagined him dead. He was dead before I was even born.

KIERAN: Maybe it's a beautiful thing—seeing your dad like that.

ZOE: There were others—people who aren't dead yet—only in the dream they were. I knew their internal organs were turning liquid, like soup.

KIERAN: Zoe—

ZOE: Then I saw you and me sprawled out. Dead. Our bodies were rotting… liquefying and gelatinous, like a stain on the concrete.

KIERAN: Oh, Zoe. We're not dead. Look at us.

ZOE: But we will die. That's the truth of it.

KIERAN: We won't die.

ZOE: One day.

KIERAN: But not now. Here we are—alive.

> *He wraps his arms around her.*

Don't have dreams like that. Wake me up next time. Promise?

ZOE: Nothing you can do about what goes in my head. The ugly thoughts filling up my head.

> KIERAN *kisses all over her forehead.*

KIERAN: If I could make them go away, I would. I would.

> ZOE *continues to shake, lost in the ugly images.*

Maybe I should've never brought you to Sydney.

ZOE: What? You make it sound like I'm some silly, little girl you led astray.

KIERAN: No, no, I never said—

ZOE: I wanted to come here, didn't I?

KIERAN: You did.

ZOE: I wanted to meet your friends, see things, do stuff. Don't you make it sound like I'm some little girl who can't handle the big, nasty world.

KIERAN: Zoe… I'm not doing that. Why are you saying this stuff?

ZOE: That's what you think, isn't it? That I'm some hopeless—

KIERAN: No, no. But we should've kept it just you and me. This place isn't right for us. We never had fights before.

ZOE: You think I've wrecked everything. You're saying—

KIERAN: No! What do you want me to say? Fuck, Zoe. Fuck.

> KIERAN's *flare of anger hits* ZOE *like a blow.*

ZOE: You hate me.

KIERAN: Don't talk shit. I don't.

ZOE: Yeah. You hate me.

KIERAN: I don't know what you want to do. One minute you want to BASE-jump off the tallest building in the universe—

ZOE: And the next minute I'm too scared to go out the door.

KIERAN: Yeah. I guess. Yeah. And the times when you get down, I never know if it's my fault or—

ZOE: It's everything. Hating myself… people being so disgusting… feeling like I can't handle anything.

KIERAN: Should I take you back home?

ZOE: I knew it. You want to get rid of me. You wish you'd never laid eyes on me.

KIERAN: No, no, the day I laid eyes on you was the most perfect day— the day I realised something could be so good.

> ZOE *goes over to him.*

ZOE: I'm sorry.

KIERAN: You're not sorry you ever came with me?

ZOE: No, no, no. I wouldn't want to miss out on anything.

KIERAN: Oh, baby, you're cold. Hey—we'll head north. Get ourselves back into a proper rhythm. Person's gotta have some sunlight on their body. We'll drive right up the coast. Yeah?

ZOE: But the car…

KIERAN: Yeah. Sheena's car's stuffed. We need a car that can get us where we need to go. And cash for petrol and whatever. I'll talk to Mick. He always knows how to get money together fast. We'll head north, make it good again.

> KIERAN *folds* ZOE *against him as they exit.*
>
> CELIA, DOROTHY *and* SHEENA *are still onstage. All three address the audience.*

CELIA: Early on, the emails that came drove me crazy. No idea where they came from.

DOROTHY: Messages from nowhere.

CELIA: But at least I would know she was alive.

SHEENA: Mum rang me. To say the police had turned up at her place.

DOROTHY: Looking for Kieran.

SHEENA: The cops found my car dumped on a street way out past Liverpool. I had to head back to Sydney to sort it out.

SHEENA *exits.*

DOROTHY: The emails from Zoe stopped coming. Then one night I saw headlights pass my house. Celia driving back alone. She is staying inside the house now since three weeks.

CELIA: I used to love the smell of winter here—the windbreak pine trees sharp and clean. Now the smell makes me nauseous. When I first came back, people dropped by to check on me. I pretended to be asleep. I couldn't bear trying to act like a normal person. Now I can hibernate undisturbed because no one comes. I check for emails. Nothing. The earth's crust has split open and sucked my daughter down where I can't find her.

CELIA *goes inside the house.*

♦ ♦ ♦ ♦ ♦

SCENE THREE

Daytime.

JOE *waits in a pub.* SHEENA *enters.*

SHEENA: Hi.

JOE: Hi.

They are awkward, not sure how to approach each other. JOE *lurches forward to give her a peck on the cheek.*

Thanks for meeting me.

SHEENA: Mum's de facto said you rang the house.

JOE: I didn't know how else to find you.

SHEENA: Well, y'know… it's fine. How's Celia?

JOE: Not good. That's why I'm here. Have you had any contact with Kieran?

SHEENA: No. But the cops came to see me yesterday.

JOE: Wanting to find him?

SHEENA: Yeah. They found his fingerprints at a break-and-enter.

JOE: In Sydney?

SHEENA: Just out of Sydney. One of those huge, show-offy houses on ten acres. The place'd been really trashed. Owner's two dogs had their skulls smashed in with a brick.

JOE: Did the police say anything about Zoe?

SHEENA: They mentioned a girl but they wouldn't tell me anything else. Mystic Sheena has a feeling in her bones it has something to do with Mick the Scumbag.

JOE: And you have no idea where Kieran is now?

SHEENA: No. I could look for him. Talk him into handing himself in to the cops before things get any worse.

JOE: I think that's a good idea. When Kieran needs legal help, call me, won't you?

SHEENA: You don't have to feel like you owe me anything.

JOE: Kieran will need help. I'm able to offer some. That's all.

> SHEENA *looks at him, then nods.*

SHEENA: Thanks.

> *An awkward silence.*

JOE: Fiona and I have separated. I've moved out.

SHEENA: Oh.

JOE: It was a long time coming, really.

SHEENA: Fair enough.

JOE: Anyway, look, I'm going to see what I can find out about Zoe. If you hear anything, please let me know.

SHEENA: Sure. I wouldn't get your hopes up. Zoe might not want to be found.

JOE: No. But I have to try. Any information is going to make it easier for Celia.

> SHEENA *looks at* JOE.

[*Rattled*] What?

SHEENA: I get it. You came here because you're looking after Celia. She's the reason.

JOE: Oh… yes, in a way, but also—

SHEENA: No, no, don't apologise for it. It's nice. Be nice to have someone to look out for you. I mean, everyone wants that.

JOE: Yeah.

> SHEENA *pulls a face then shrugs.*

SHEENA: Anyway, I'll check out the scabby palaces my brother crashes in. I'll call you if I find anything.

SHEENA *exits, then* JOE.

◆ ◆ ◆ ◆ ◆

SCENE FOUR

Daytime. The peach farm.

DOROTHY *enters with a basket of food containers.*

DOROTHY: [*to the audience*] I leave food on the doorstep every day. Celia eats enough to live. [*She looks towards the shack.*] Early this morning, I'm thinking I saw something moving near the shack. But then I think, 'Dorothy, the dementia is getting you now, old chicken'.

    There is a sound from the shack.

[*Calling*] Celia! Celia! Come quickly! Someone is here, I think. [*She approaches the shack.*] Hello? Are you there, someone? Or are you

Maggie Blinco as Dorothy in the 2006 Griffin Theatre Company production in Sydney. (Photo: Robert McFarlane)

an animal?

CELIA *emerges from the house, squinting against the bright daylight.*

CELIA: Dorothy, what's going on?

DOROTHY *points to the shack just as we hear more noise.*

Who's there? Zoe? Is someone there?

DOROTHY: [*to the audience*] You could see how much she was hoping. Oh, don't hope too much.

All goes quiet.

CELIA: Both of us are imagining things that aren't there.

CELIA *turns to go back inside.*

DOROTHY: [*to the audience*] Then the hope is gone and that's even worse.

There is another noise from the shack. CELIA *grabs a lump of wood as a weapon.*

CELIA: Zoe? If there's someone there, come out.

KIERAN *comes out. He's filthy, his face battered and scabbed from recent injuries, frantic, barely coherent.*

Where's Zoe?

KIERAN: Is she here?

CELIA: Where is she? Tell me where she is!

KIERAN: I don't know. I thought she'd come home—is she here?

CELIA: No! When did you last see her? Did she say she was coming home?

KIERAN: No. I don't know where she is. That's why I— Is she here?

CELIA: I told you no.

KIERAN *paces aimlessly, winding himself up.*

KIERAN: Where is she? Fuck. Fuck.

CELIA: Listen to me, you little piece of shit, you tell me right now where I can find her.

KIERAN: I don't know.

CELIA: Where did you last see her?

KIERAN: Sydney—well, near Sydney. But then she disappeared.

CELIA: Give me a list of places I can look.

KIERAN: I already looked every place I could think. If I knew where she was I wouldn't be here. That's why I'm— You're trying to trick me… asking me— She's really inside, isn't she?

> CELIA *shakes her head.*

She's in there and you won't let me see her. [*Calling past* CELIA *to the house*] Zoe! Zoe! It's me! [*To* CELIA] I just wanna talk to her. Please. Let me talk to her.

CELIA: I told you—

KIERAN: She's inside. She's asleep in bed, tucked up in bed in her old room, isn't she?

CELIA: No. She's not.

> *The wretched way* CELIA *says it gets through to him.*

KIERAN: Oh… she's really not here.

DOROTHY: No.

CELIA: The last time you saw Zoe, she was okay? She was in one piece?

KIERAN: Yes. Yes.

CELIA: Where is she now? Do you know where?

KIERAN: [*shaking his head*] I'll wait for her. She'll come back home. If I had a place like this—I'd come back here. I'll wait.

CELIA: Get off my property. I don't want you anywhere near this place.

KIERAN: I can see why you hate me. But I can't go. I have to see her.

CELIA: If you don't get off my property right now, I'll ring the police.

KIERAN: That might make trouble with the cops for Zoe. I know you don't want that.

CELIA: Just get out of here, you little shit. I don't want to see you. Get out of here!

KIERAN: [*backing away*] I'll get off your property. But I can't go away. She'll come back here. I'm sorry to be a shit. But I'll do whatever I have to do to see her. You can't make me go away.

CELIA: Get out of here! Go!

> KIERAN *runs off.*

I should go to Sydney. Find her.

DOROTHY: Where? The boy can't give you any useful information. Look at him.

CELIA: No, but—

DOROTHY: What if the boy is right? What if Zoe comes back here but you're gone?

CELIA: He seems so sure she's coming home.

DOROTHY: He does.

> CELIA *exits.*

[*To the audience*] For two days and two nights, the boy waited on the roadside near the gate. He was drenched with rain, bitten by the morning frost. But he did not budge himself. I heard Celia shout at him, 'Go away!' Like a person snarling at a stray dog. But Kieran didn't budge himself. I offered him a bed for the night at my house. He said, 'Thank you, but no'. He was afraid that if he moved from his watching spot, he would miss Zoe coming home. I think too that the biting rain, his poor, battered face, Celia's vicious shouting—the boy thought he deserved this kind of punishment.

> CELIA *comes out of the house, peering down the road.*

[*To* CELIA] The boy wants to ask you a question.

> CELIA *doesn't respond, hard-faced.*

DOROTHY: Two nights he's been out there.

CELIA: If I could get the police to drag him away, I would.

DOROTHY: But all he wants—

CELIA: If he can't help me find her, he's no use to me.

> DOROTHY *signals to* KIERAN *at the gate.*

DOROTHY: [*calling*] Kieran! Come up here! Kieran! [*To the audience*] People might say I was an interfering, old, mad lady. Sometimes old, mad ladies should interfere.

> KIERAN *enters.* DOROTHY *gestures to him to address* CELIA.

KIERAN: I was wondering if… Has Zoe called you?

CELIA: No.

KIERAN: You don't have to tell me if she's called. I mean, that's your right.

CELIA: She hasn't called.

KIERAN: I should've talked her into calling. I'm really sorry.

CELIA: Are you?

KIERAN: Yes. Yes. I'm so sorry. I stuffed everything up. I know that.

CELIA: Why did you and Zoe get separated?

KIERAN: Because I'm such an idiot. I wreck everything. I don't mean to but I make dumb, dumb, dumb mistakes and… it all gets stuffed up.

KIERAN, *in his distress, rubs and pulls at his face.*

CELIA: Don't do that. You're making yourself bleed.

KIERAN: I'm sorry, y'know… I'm really sorry.

CELIA: Hey. Hey. Look what you're doing.

She grabs one of his hands to pull it away from his face.

Don't do that to yourself.

KIERAN *looks at his hands, bloody from the reopened injuries.*

What happened to your face?

KIERAN: Oh, I… uh… I fell.

CELIA: Above your eye should have been stitched.

KIERAN *sways a little, groggy.*

Sit down a minute. Don't fall over.

KIERAN: Not eating, I guess.

CELIA: Sit down for a minute.

Meanwhile DOROTHY *has fetched a first-aid kit from the shed.*

DOROTHY: You can use this.

KIERAN *sits on a pile of palettes and* CELIA *cleans up the cuts on his face and puts on steri-strips.*

CELIA: Keep still.

KIERAN *is still and obedient as she works.*

This might sting.

KIERAN: No worries. Thanks. Already hurts anyway. Thanks.

CELIA: When you last saw Zoe, how was she?

KIERAN: I don't want you to think it was always bad. To begin with, things were great. Me and Zoe looked after each other and we—

CELIA: Where did you go when you first left here?

KIERAN: All over. Looking for picking work.

CELIA: You got work?

KIERAN: Yeah. We lived out of the car which was fine because it was warm enough to sleep out. Plenty of amazing fruit around to eat— right there in front of us. So we ate healthy and found rivers to swim in and stayed away from trouble. I want you to know that. No trouble.

CELIA: You said something about the police.

KIERAN: Well, yeah, yeah… But until things went bad, it was good.

CELIA: Why did you give up the picking?

KIERAN: No matter where we went, Zoe could suss people out really quick. She's excellent at talking to people, isn't she? She's so smart.

CELIA: Do you think she's in Sydney now?

> KIERAN *is too sleepy to answer.* CELIA *lets him flop back and close his eyes as she exits.*

DOROTHY: [*to the audience*] Celia let the boy sleep that night in the shack.

> CELIA *re-enters and hands* KIERAN *a clean t-shirt.*

CELIA: Clean yourself up.

> KIERAN *retreats and changes his shirt.* CELIA *stays in the yard, staring down towards the road.*

DOROTHY: [*to the audience*] The boy hanged around but watchful, like a dog that is worried it might get a sharp kick any minute. Celia, she was tearing between the urge to smash at this boy and her need to hear him talk about Zoe.

> KIERAN *ventures closer but keeping out of* CELIA*'s way.*

CELIA: When Zoe wanted to go to Sydney, what was in her mind? Did she say what she—?

KIERAN: 'Dive into everything headfirst'—that's what she said. Oh, I'm not making excuses. I should've known it was a bad idea.

CELIA: Why?

KIERAN: Things went off the rails. My fault. And Zoe started getting really down.

CELIA: Down?

KIERAN: Sometimes she'd get so dark. I'd say, 'Come on, Zoe, we're the lucky ones'. I've seen people be slack or straight-out cruel to the exact people they're supposed to be looking after. I knew what me and Zoe had was good—because I've seen the other ways it can be. But some days she'd sink into a black hole so deep you couldn't even yell down to her. That's why I panicked. I didn't think straight… I stuffed up.

> KIERAN *starts to cry.*

CELIA: What happened?

> KIERAN *crumples at* CELIA'*s feet.*

KIERAN: You gotta believe I'd never do anything to hurt Zoe. I thought we could look after each other. Please believe me. I'm sorry. I'm sorry.

> CELIA *stares down at the boy sobbing at her feet. Eventually she reaches out, touching his hair. He grabs onto her legs and she freezes, startled. Then she leans down to rub circles on his back, like someone soothing a young child. Finally, she helps him to his feet and leads him inside the house.*

DOROTHY: [*to the audience*] The boy cried for a long time. Big sobs tearing out from his belly. Celia could not ask any more questions. Eventually he cried himself to sleep on the couch and she covered him with a blanket.

◆ ◆ ◆ ◆ ◆

SCENE FIVE

A Sydney house.

SHEENA *enters, carrying a supermarket bag with bottles and packets in it. She kneels down on the floor next to a mattress where* ZOE *is asleep, covered in a blanket.* SHEENA *checks* ZOE'*s forehead, tucks the blanket around her more snugly and waits.*

ZOE *stirs awake. She's dark-eyed, weak, febrile.*

SHEENA: Gets noisy in his house once the trucks start.

> *She pours Lucozade into a coffee mug and helps* ZOE *drink, then swallow two aspirin.*

Temperature's down a bit compared to last night. Drink more of the Lucozade. The chemist said it's good stuff when a person's rundown.

ZOE: I don't understand… how come you—?

SHEENA: I was looking for Kieran. Found you.

ZOE: I don't get why you're helping me. You hate me. You think I'm some—

SHEENA: I think you're a selfish, little bitch who doesn't have any clue how lucky she is. You deserve to sit in your own mess.

ZOE: I know you blame me about Kieran… and you're right.

SHEENA: Don't flatter yourself, sweetheart. Kieran would've got himself into major shit without any inspiration from you.

ZOE: It's my fault we broke into that house with the dogs. Kieran only went along with Mick because he wanted to get some money together. To take me up the coast. Mick knew where this guy kept big rolls of cash.

SHEENA: Why did Kieran take you with them?

ZOE: I wanted to make sure it didn't get out of hand.

SHEENA: But you can't stop a creature like Mick.

> ZOE *shakes her head. She describes everything like it's a dark dream.*

ZOE: 'Don't worry. Mick's just a bit amped up.' That's what Kieran said—before. We got inside… Mick started smashing things with a crowbar. Set the alarms off. Kieran's yelling at him—upset about what Mick did to the dogs. Mick got even more aggro… like someone'd flicked a switch in his brain. Mick's girlfriend—Jade— she was there too. Jade was screaming and he hit her with his fist— so hard she slammed into the edge of a table—here. [*Indicating her abdomen*] The look on Mick's face at the moment he hit her. I can't describe it.

SHEENA: I can imagine.

> ZOE *looks at* SHEENA. *Maybe* SHEENA *can imagine.*

ZOE: Kieran put himself in front of Mick. 'Stop it, Mick. Calm down.' Mick thumps him down, pushes Kieran's face into the broken glass. Kieran couldn't see… because of the blood on his face. Mick's yelling nonstop for everyone to shut up. He looks straight at me… his eyes… like he wasn't a human being anymore. I was on the floor. Mick jammed down the heel of his hand here— [*Indicating her neck*] I felt the weight of him pressing on my throat. This is it. He's killing me. I'm going to die right now. But then the pressure of his hand weakened for a second… I rolled sideways… I had to get away. I ran and Jade did too. We ran across a paddock until we got to a school bus shelter. Jade had bad pain where she hit the table.

I said we should go to a hospital but she wanted to lie down for a while first. It was so good to close my eyes, somewhere quiet. I must've fallen asleep. When I woke up, it was cold. I touched Jade's arm, whispered in case she was asleep—'Does it still hurt?' Her skin felt like plastic. She was dead. Right beside me on the bench.

> ZOE *and* SHEENA *sit in silence for a moment.* SHEENA *refills the mug with Lucozade.*

SHEENA: You look terrible. Keep drinking this stuff.

> JOE *calls from outside.*

JOE: [*offstage*] Sheena?

SHEENA: In here!

ZOE: Joe… is that Joe?

SHEENA: I rang him.

> JOE *enters and goes straight to enfold* ZOE.

JOE: Zoe. Are you okay? You feel feverish. Are you all right?

ZOE: I'm all right.

SHEENA: She needs to see a doctor.

JOE: Yes. We'll get you to a doctor. Oh, Zoe… it's so wonderful to see you. [*To* SHEENA] She's okay?

SHEENA: Not pregnant, not addicted to heroin, alive.

JOE: Thanks, Sheena. For taking care of her.

SHEENA: I just found her.

JOE: [*to* ZOE] It's going to be difficult for me to ever forgive you. If you weren't so sick right now, I'd shake you hard. I'd shake the teeth right out of your stupid head.

ZOE: I tried to ring. Couldn't ever do it. I was scared if I heard her voice, I'd—I don't know…

JOE: It was cruel, Zoe.

ZOE: I didn't think…

JOE: So cruel.

ZOE: I'm sorry.

> JOE *rushes to hug her, as* ZOE *crumples into tears.*

JOE: It's so good to see you. Let's get you home.

ZOE: I can't go home. There'd be too much. I can't do it.

JOE: She'll want to see you so badly.

ZOE: You understand why, don't you, Sheena?

SHEENA: I think I do.

ZOE: How can I describe things to her? I can't. I can't face her.

SHEENA: Yeah, you can. Go home.

JOE: Let me drive you home.

ZOE: [*to* SHEENA] Would you come with me?

SHEENA: Oh… I don't think that's a good idea. What difference would it make if—?

ZOE: I know you understand things. It would just feel right… easier.

SHEENA: No, look, Joe can take you back.

JOE: It'd be helpful if you come along and look after Zoe— I mean, if you—

ZOE: Please, Sheena.

SHEENA: If you want.

> JOE *and* SHEENA *stand either side of* ZOE *to steady her as they walk out.*

◆ ◆ ◆ ◆ ◆

SCENE SIX

Late afternoon. The farm.

CELIA *and* DOROTHY *are in the yard.*

DOROTHY: [*to the audience*] In the last two days, the boy has begun to do jobs around the farm, fixing things, on his own accord—as if this earns the right to stay. Today he is in the orchard clearing weeds.

> *As soon as* CELIA *sees* JOE *approach, she's breathless, overwhelmed.*

JOE: Don't panic when you see her. She's sick, but she's all right.

> ZOE *enters, steadied by* SHEENA. CELIA *hurries towards her and* ZOE *runs the last few steps to meet* CELIA. *They hang onto each other, weeping,* CELIA *sometimes laughing with disbelief.* CELIA *holds* ZOE *away a little, so she can look at her, then folds her in close again.*

CELIA: Dorothy. Where did he go?

> DOROTHY *indicates the orchard.*

ZOE: Who?

CELIA: Kieran's here.

SHEENA: He's alive?

DOROTHY: Working at the far end of the orchard.

CELIA: Call him.

DOROTHY: [*calling*] Kieran! Kieran!

> ZOE *runs closer to the orchard, watching* KIERAN *approach.*

[*To the audience*] There are things you can solve by throwing effort at them, by doing something. But some necessary things—like letting your child go out into the world—the beautiful, perilous world—require you just to sit. Sit with things gnawing in your belly and learn not to do anything.

> KIERAN *emerges from the orchard. He and* ZOE *fly into each other's arms, kissing and apologising, talking over each other.*

ZOE: I'm sorry I said those things. I never meant those things.

KIERAN: I thought Mick was gonna kill you. I stuffed up. Everything.

ZOE: No. That's not true.

KIERAN: I dragged you down.

ZOE: No. Don't say that. I'm sorry I ran. I was sorry straight away. But then I couldn't find you.

KIERAN: I got so worried. I went looking for you.

ZOE: I thought you'd given up on me.

KIERAN: No, no, I was looking. That's why I came here. I thought you'd come home.

ZOE: I ended up at Mick's house last. I thought you'd go back there.

KIERAN: I'm sorry. That's my fault. I'm sorry. You're shivering. Keep warm.

> KIERAN *wraps his jacket around* ZOE *and leads her towards* CELIA.

ZOE: I need to lie down. Here is good. [*She climbs up to stretch out on a stack of palettes.*] I'm okay. Just need to sleep.

CELIA: I think so.

KIERAN: You'll be okay, now. You'll be looked after, now.

ZOE: Things are in a mess, Mum… I can't think properly…

> CELIA *climbs up on the palettes so* ZOE *can rest her head in* CELIA'*s lap.*

CELIA: We'll work it out. Tonight you sleep, and in the morning you'll be able to think.

> ZOE *lies with her head in* CELIA*'s lap, with* CELIA *stroking the hair back from her forehead.* ZOE *falls asleep.*

Sheena. Thank you so much. For bringing her home.

SHEENA: You're welcome.

CELIA: Stay the night here, won't you?

SHEENA: Oh, well—

CELIA: Please.

SHEENA: Okay. Ta.

> SHEENA *is still and impassive as* KIERAN *bounds up to her.*

KIERAN: Sheena, it's so great to see you!

> SHEENA *slaps his face hard.*

Yeah. Yeah. Fair enough. I deserve that. Have you been good? Have you been—?

> *She slaps him hard again.*

Okay, Sheena. I reckon you've got a right to do that. You got every right to be—

> SHEENA *raises her hand to slap again, but this time* KIERAN *ducks away.*

I'm sorry if you were worried about me.

SHEENA: I wasn't.

KIERAN: Yeah? Good. Great.

SHEENA: I decided months ago not to give a flying fuck about you anymore.

KIERAN: Yep. I can see why. Excellent decision. Good one.

SHEENA: I should've let you get yourself arrested last year.

KIERAN: You probably should've.

SHEENA: I should've left you to clean up your own filthy messes.

KIERAN: Maybe that's right.

SHEENA: I should've walked away three years ago when you were frying your brain with chemicals.

KIERAN: Maybe.

SHEENA: I should've left you to kill yourself.

KIERAN: I'm glad you didn't.

SHEENA *shrugs then looks away.*

How are you, Sheena? Be happy. I want you to be happy. I wish I could give you that.

SHEENA: Well, you can't.

KIERAN: Nah, making Crankypants happy is beyond even the powers of a legend like me.

SHEENA *smiles despite herself.*

Ha! A smile! Or nearly. I can do that. Which is not much. Not a tiny, fucking scrap of what you deserve, Sheena.

SHEENA: Just shut up for a second, Kieran. Can you do that?

KIERAN: I can do that.

KIERAN *and* SHEENA *sit together.*

JOE *goes over to* CELIA, *who has* ZOE *curled in her lap.*

JOE: Is she asleep? Should we carry her in to bed?

CELIA: In a minute.

JOE *nods, seeing how happy* CELIA *is like that.*

JOE: Don't worry about police and any of that tonight. I'll find out more. Find out where we stand.

CELIA: You're a good friend to us, Joe.

JOE *shrugs, smiles.*

Maybe I should've locked her in a room for a few years. There are parents who do that. Until social workers break into the house years later and find the children squinting against daylight.

JOE *looks at her.*

I'm joking.

JOE: I realise that.

CELIA: What do I do now?

JOE: I don't know. I guess I think you've gotta ask yourself what you want. Do you want Zoe to throw herself into the things she loves with all her soul?

CELIA: Yes.

JOE: But you never want her to experience misery or failure.

CELIA: No.

JOE: Do you want her to travel the world and see mind-blowing things?

CELIA: Yes.

JOE: And have lots of intense, spontaneous, unpredictable moments in her life?

CELIA: Yes.

JOE: But you don't want her to face any possibility of pain.

CELIA: No.

JOE: Can you hear what you're—?

CELIA: Yes.

They exchange a smile.

JOE: Anyway, it's good to see you looking— You've been so unhappy and I can't bear to see that.

She smiles, surprised by his intimate tone.

CELIA: It's getting cold out here. Can you help me carry her inside?

JOE and CELIA carry ZOE inside. KIERAN doesn't take his eyes off ZOE until she's gone.

SHEENA: Where's Mick now?

KIERAN: Shot through. He knew some guys in WA. He might've gone there.

SHEENA: Will the police blame you for all of it? And what happened to Jade?

KIERAN: Oh. Hadn't thought of that. Maybe. Poor Jade.

SHEENA: I can't get you out of this one, Kieran.

KIERAN: I know that. Yep. I made this stuff-up and I'm gonna have to wear it.

SHEENA: Even if I wanted to, there's nothing I can do.

KIERAN looks to the spot where ZOE was sleeping a moment ago.

KIERAN: She's so beautiful... so beautiful. None of that muck should've ever touched her. [*Jumping to his feet, suddenly wired up*] You know what I should do?

SHEENA: Get a good night's sleep and in the morning ask Joe for proper advice on—

KIERAN: No, no. I've gotta fix it so Zoe doesn't get dragged down into any of it. I'll go to the cops... in Sydney, right away from here. They don't ever have to know Zoe was with me. I'll say it was just me and Mick.

SHEENA: Kieran. Hold on.

KIERAN: No, no, don't you get it? This way, Zoe doesn't get tangled up in it. This is the right thing to do.

SHEENA: But you gotta make sure it's the right thing for you, mate. What if the cops never get hold of Mick, they might blame you for—

KIERAN: Doesn't matter. I have to do this—before anyone talks me out of it.

SHEENA: If this is a mistake, don't expect me to bail you out or feel bad for you.

KIERAN: I don't.

SHEENA *looks at him for a moment, then gets her wallet out.*

SHEENA: Sixty-five bucks. That's all I've got.

KIERAN: Ta. I can hitch, get to a bus or a train.

SHEENA *gives him the money as they exit.*

Night falls.

DOROTHY: [*to the audience*] The boy waited until everyone was asleep. Then he headed off. I saw the headlights of a truck cut through the dark at the crossroads. I saw the truck stop to give the boy a lift. But the rest were deep asleep.

◆ ◆ ◆ ◆ ◆

SCENE SEVEN

Dawn.

CELIA *emerges from the house, stretching, happy.* SHEENA *wanders in from the orchard.*

SHEENA: Good morning.

CELIA: Reckon I had the deepest, sweetest sleep I've had in months— no, years.

ZOE *comes outside, a quilt wrapped around her.*

How are you feeling?

ZOE: Better.

CELIA: There's colour in your face again.

ZOE: Is Kieran awake?

SHEENA: He's gone. Hitched to Sydney.

ZOE: What?

SHEENA: He's gone to turn himself in. He wants to keep Zoe out of it completely. The police don't have to know she was ever there.

ZOE: What? Why?

SHEENA: He wants to protect you. Keep you away from all of it.

ZOE: Who told him to do that?

SHEENA: No one. He decided it's the right thing to do.

ZOE: It's a dumb thing to do! Shit... I can't believe he'd— Why didn't you talk him out of it? Why didn't you make him wait until—?

SHEENA: He wants to do the right thing.

ZOE: But this is crazy! Mum, tell her it's a stupid idea.

> CELIA *doesn't respond.*

SHEENA: Y'know, it's not a stupid idea. Kieran's in deep trouble anyway. Doesn't mean you have to be.

ZOE: No no, this is not right... no way... For one thing, I can tell the police what really happened. What if Kieran gets blamed for everything? I can tell them it was Mick. That it wasn't all Kieran.

SHEENA: He wants to save you from that mess. [*To* CELIA] Explain to her why this is a reasonable idea. Why should she be dragged down into it if she doesn't have to be?

ZOE: You don't think that, do you, Mum?

SHEENA: She can stay here. No one ever has to know she was anywhere near that place.

ZOE: I was there. I was with the girl who died. I have to go and tell what happened. Don't you think? Mum? Mum?

> CELIA *is silent, not revealing her response.*

I can't hide here and pretend nothing ever happened.

CELIA: Well, I think—

ZOE: I should go to the police, say what happened.

CELIA: Yes. If that's what you want to do, I'll drive you into town.

ZOE: Yes. Please.

◆ ◆ ◆ ◆ ◆

SCENE EIGHT

The glare of a hot summer day.

Bins full of peaches. Harvest is in full swing. CELIA *is working hard.*

DOROTHY: This summer, our old pickers are back. Not so much fruit to pick—because of Celia letting the trees go in ruin last winter.

> JOE *enters. He kisses* DOROTHY *hello.*

JOE: I dropped another carload of boxes on your back porch.

DOROTHY: [*to the audience*] Josef is moving in with me—just for this autumn while he renovates the house he bought in town. [*To* CELIA] Have you laid your eyes on the ugly, fibro hovel?

CELIA: Not yet.

DOROTHY: What can you say when you discover your child has no taste? Sandor and I brought him up looking at books about the great cities and their fine buildings, appreciating what is well-proportioned and elegant.

CELIA: And yet now he buys an ugly house.

DOROTHY: Celia, we are talking make-you-want-to-slit-your-throat ugly.

JOE: I explained to you that it's a matter of—

DOROTHY: None of my business. I keep my mouth shut.

> ZOE *comes out of the orchard. Hot and sweaty, she stops to guzzle water and trickle some over her face and neck.*

[*To the audience*] Zoe goes now to a school in the city, living with her aunt. Celia has had her home for the summer. Today she leaves us again to go back. Zoe went to court and has what is called a 'good behaviour bond' on her. Hunh—I don't know so many people who would last long if they were supposed to have always good behaviour. Kieran, he spent some time in prison. Zoe and the boy do the email to each other.

> CELIA *and* JOE *watch* ZOE *down by the orchard.*

CELIA: It's lovely, you driving Zoe back.

JOE: I've got meetings in the city. I can drop her off on my way.

CELIA: Zoe's all packed. Suitcase by the door.

JOE: She does want to go back to Sydney?

CELIA: Yes, mostly. There are so many good reasons for her to be there.

JOE: I had a call from Sheena this morning.

CELIA: Oh. I didn't know you—uh—

JOE: Just sorting out the last of the legal mess. She has a new bloke apparently.

CELIA: And is this new bloke—?

JOE: Not a total dropkick, it seems.

CELIA: I hope that's right.

JOE: She said Kieran's heading to the Northern Territory.

CELIA: According to Zoe, he wants to go up there, look for work, clear his head.

JOE: I think it's a good idea.

CELIA: Yes.

DOROTHY: [*to the audience*] Who can say what will happen to that boy at the long run? Me, I see perhaps bad things for a boy like that—rolling his car on a dirt road… stumbling into the path of some angry man at the worst moment… you know. But I can't see into the future. Some people might join me in my hoping for the best for that boy.

CELIA: Oh, Joe, look at the time. You need to get on the road.

JOE: No rush. So I'm late for the meeting. I'll put her suitcase in the car.

> JOE *exits to the house.*

DOROTHY: [*to the audience*] So. It seems no vodka for me this winter— since I'll have my son living with me. Josef can help around this place and he can help me keep Celia company when Zoe's gone back to the city.

> CELIA, *looking down at* ZOE, *addresses the audience.*

CELIA: [*to the audience*] I can see that Zoe is stronger. She doesn't let unimportant things get to her like she used to. But sometimes, when we talk on the phone, it only takes two syllables and I can hear if she's wretched. That blackness in her voice.

DOROTHY: [*to the audience*] The worrying doesn't stop.

CELIA: [*to the audience*] At night I still catalogue dangers, but now I add to the conjured scenes. I rewrite the stories—imagine Zoe escaping trouble by her good judgement, quick wits, strong heart.

DOROTHY: [*to the audience*] There is comfort in that.

CELIA: [*to the audience*] I urge her to be strong. As if all my hours of worrying and urging will distil and harden into a small, bright amulet she can wear around her neck to protect her wherever she is.

ZOE *waves up to her mother.*

ZOE: Mum! Do I need to come and get ready now?

CELIA: Soon.

ZOE *stretches, then mimes that her back and shoulders are killing her.* CELIA *laughs, adoring her.*

THE END

PRAISE FOR THE PEACH SEASON

'Like Oswald's parable *Mr Bailey's Minder*, *The Peach Season* is about the redemption of damaged souls who have lost their nerve or crave adventure. It combines deadpan humour, emotional truths and gusto … the virtue of Oswald's funny and tender play is that it's deeply caring of people, irrespective of the mess they create or get themselves into.' *Sydney Morning Herald*

'Like her earlier plays *Gary's House* and *Sweet Road*, *The Peach Season* is about people on the run, moving about the country trying to find peace, meeting each other and making connections … Debra Oswald does this sort of deeply human comedy-drama superbly well … an emotional and sometimes very funny story.' The *Australian*

'David Berthold is making his mark on Sydney theatre with his repertoire at Griffin, and he has directed this play with care for its emotional nuances.' The *Australian*

ALSO BY DEBRA OSWALD

Dags

Gilliam is 16, suffers from the occasional 'ack-attack' and is worried about not having a boyfriend. She loves chocolate and gelato, and is infatuated with the best-looking boy in school. *Dags* is a funny and compassionate look at the trials of adolescence: pimples, heartache and self-discovery.
ISBN 978 086819 1805

Gary's House

Gary has failed in everything he has attempted. But when he inherits a block of land, he gets an urge to build a nest with Sue-Ann, his angry and pregnant girlfriend. *Gary's House* is a story about Aussie battlers—battling with each other, the elements and the world in their quest to turn a dream into reality. What begins as satire becomes a moving drama told with humour, compassion and loving detail by a highly original and insightful playwright.
ISBN 978 086819 6077

Mr Bailey's Minder

Abusive, cantankerous and burned out by booze, Leo Bailey is one of Australia's national treasures. A gifted painter and chronic alcoholic, he can no longer take care of himself. His resentful daughter has been through a succession of minders, until Therese comes along, fresh out of jail and determined to make a go of her limited options. *My Bailey's Minder* is a tough, funny and big-hearted play. It's about shame and judgement, about who deserves to be loved and forgiven. It looks at how people exploit each other and where they find the beauty; and the qualities of transcendence, letting go and forgiveness.
ISBN 978 086819 7616

Skate

Any plans for a skate park in Narragindi are dead in the water. The kids of the town are left to skate on the town hall steps and take their chances avoiding the local police. Zac, a young leader among the many youth committees set up to get a skate park, wants no part in another attempt. His best mate, Corey, a guy with a troubled history, has a passion for the new campaign, sparked by his interest in Lauren, a member of the new committee. When tragedy strikes, the town is galvanised into action, and what was originally a fight for a skate park grows into a struggle for acceptance and unity. *Skate* is a turbo-charged, moving and funny account of the mates, mothers, tricks and traumas of a group of young skaters. Enhanced by live skateboarding, the play is full of the emotional awkwardness of adolescence, its adrenalin, compassion and humour, and reflects the hopes and aspirations of young people in regional Australia.
ISBN 978 086819 7272

Sweet Road

Jo is on the road. So too are Carla, Andy, Blake, Nicole and Browndog. Along with Yasmin, Michael, Frank and Curtis, each has a plan on where they are going and a determination to get there. But as their lives interweave and disperse and plans go awry, each of them discovers that the road they are travelling may not always take them where they expected, and if they are lucky, the destination may be more wonderful than any of them could ever have dreamed. Full of vitality and good humour, *Sweet Road* is a play which explores the aspirations and idiosyncrasies of seemingly ordinary people as they cross the vast and far from ordinary Australian landscape.
ISBN 978 086819 6169

ALSO AVAILABLE FROM CURRENCY PRESS

Love
Patricia Cornelius
Tanya, Annie and Lorenzo are at the bottom of the heap. They're young but already the youth has been wrung out of them. They've been abused, they're abusive and they're difficult to like, let alone love. But it is love in all its distorted and mutated forms that holds them together. Annie and Tanya make a pact: their love will protect them from an unloving world and it will endure. Even the charming, dreadful Lorenzo will not threaten it. Only doubt in each other's love can put a wedge between them. Premiered by HotHouse Theatre in 2005, Patricia Cornelius's uncompromising play won the 2003 Wal Cherry Award for Play of the Year and the 2006 Australian Writers' Guild Award (AWGIE) for Best Play.
ISBN 978 086819 7944

The Blonde, the Brunette, and the Vengeful Redhead
Robert Hewett
Everyone has their own story to tell about the day that Rhonda went beserk in the shopping mall. And who's to know where the truth lies? With the best friend who might have egged her on? With the husband who denies responsibility? Or with the victim's family whose lives were changed forever? And then there's the story of the vengeful redhead herself, but she's probably the least likely to know what really happened. In this gripping adventure, the world is turned upside down in a disastrous and comic sequence of events. As the intrigue unfolds, seven different characters give a fresh twist of perspective—all played by one multi-faceted performer.
ISBN 978 086819 8064

The Nightwatchman
Daniel Keene

Giles has lived a life amongst the rambling beauty of the old family home. Now he's gone blind, and his children Hélène and Michel have returned for a few days to move him to a secure apartment. On the outside Gilles is stoic, resigned to his fate, but inside he silently rages against the darkness. Hélène feels the weight of responsibility—for both her father and her own family. The fragility of her marriage has her longing for the untroubled days of her childhood. Photographer Michel is on the verge of a quiet breakdown. Drawn together in a garden full of echoes, the three discover tender memories of a shared past unwilling to release them. 'What small elements Daniel Keene uses to conjure up his theatrical and poetic magic... It's like Samuel Beckett at his best.' John McCallum, The *Australian*
ISBN 978 086819 8019

Strangers in Between / Holding the Man (adapted from the book by Timothy Conigrave)
Tommy Murphy

Two acclaimed plays from Australia's brightest new playwright, Tommy Murphy, currently 'rocketing through the Australian theatre scene' (*Sydney Morning Herald*).

In *Strangers in Between*, Shane has fled his family and is seeking refuge in Kings Cross. Confused and naïve, he befriends two strangers and with their help—or hindrance—grapples to reconcile himself with events from his past. But how can he move on when he can't even use laundry powder? *Strangers in Between* won the 2006 Premier's Literary Award for Best Play.

Holding the Man is based on Timothy Conigrave's celebrated memoir of the same name which won the 1995 UN Human Rights Award for Non-Fiction. Tommy Murphy's stage adaptation faithfully captures the book's heart-wrenchingly honest portrayal of a fifteen-year relationship.

Speaking across generations, sexualities and cultures, both plays explore what it means to grow up, how we form relationships, and why we need to love and be loved. Features an introduction by David Berthold, director of the premiere productions of both plays.
ISBN 978 086819 7968

The Merry-go-round in the Sea
Dickon Oxenburgh and Andrew Ross
Adapted from the novel by Randolph Stow

The year is 1941, Australian soldiers are fighting overseas and air raid trenches are being dug in the backyards of Geraldton, just in case. Six-year-old Rob Coram idolises his enigmatic older cousin Rick, but his idyllic existence on the west coast of Australia is disrupted when Rick volunteers for active service. Interned by the Japanese, Rick struggles to survive, just as Rob will struggle to overcome the void created by Rick's absence and to understand the disillusioned man who returns. Adapted from Randolph Stow's classic novel, *The Merry-go-round in the Sea* captures the restless spirit of post-war Australia. Winner of the 1997 Western Australian Premier's Book Award for Best Script.
ISBN 978 086819 7883

Toby
Abe Pogos

Toby is the social outcast in a nineteenth-century European village. Robbed by his best friend, hounded by the authorities and branded a gypsy, Toby's life is somewhat dysfunctional. In desperation he hatches a plan designed to enhance his chances with the beautiful Joan and his standing in the village generally. But he uncovers more about honesty and power than he anticipated. A timely and darkly comic fable, Toby explores racism, genocide and the politics of power.
ISBN 978 086819 7333